I0699662

ILLUSION OF HAZEL

AN ALLIUM SERIES NOVELLA

MALLORY BENJAMIN

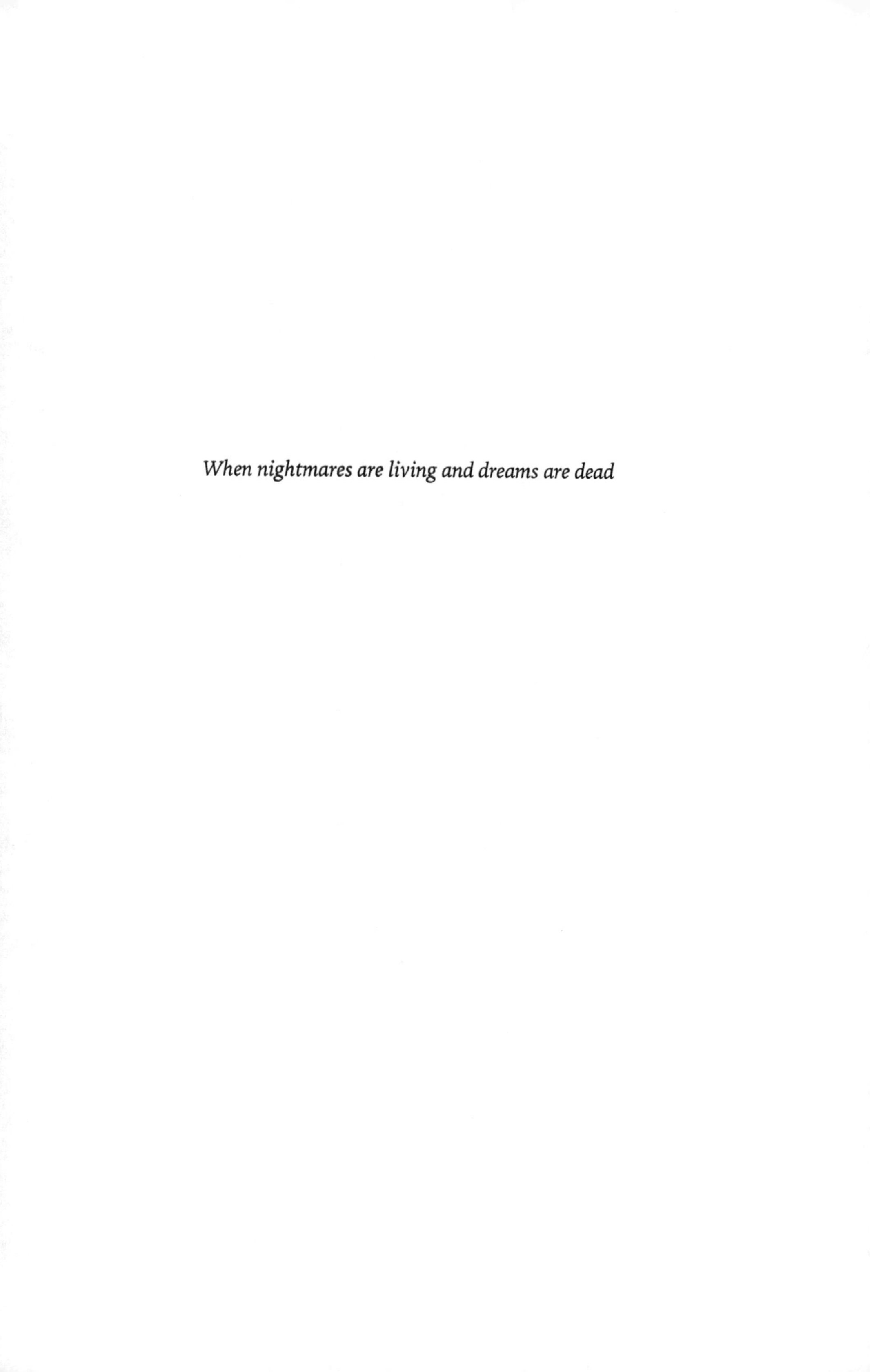

When nightmares are living and dreams are dead

NARWAY
KITLARN
THE DARK KINGDOM OF TENNEBRIS

Backerly
Palm
Addler
LakeWood

AUTHOR'S NOTE

Illusion of Hazel takes place during the duration of Lake of Sapphire and Ocean of Silver. Recommend reading after finishing Ocean of Silver.

ONE
GREYLAND

THE SUN WAS STILL BEATING DOWN on me as my father and I waited for Sie. We were in the middle of our summer season, and even though the air always had a chill, it was the warmest Tennebris ever got.

I was sweating under my clothes, not from the heat—or lack of it—but from what was about to happen. My father's smug expression told me enough about what to expect.

But Sie had no idea what was coming for him. I knew he planned on avoiding coming back to the house tonight. Hell, I'd avoid our home too if I could. It was why I was leaving for school first thing in the morning even though classes didn't start for another week. My small ass dorm room was better than our mansion whenever my father was home.

I was excited to meet my brother's future wife, but I was terrified about why my father wanted to meet her. He hated rank zeroes. He nearly broke everything in our house when Scotlind Rumor was announced as Sie's bride. My mom and I had been doing our best to avoid him, but weeks later, his rage still hadn't tempered.

I saw a flash of onyx hair right as Sie was about to enter the Kitlarn Inn. Our father started walking toward him, his boots crunching against the pebbled gravel. I silently followed. It was best not to draw attention to myself. He didn't care what I did anyway—and he wouldn't unless I became a five like my brother when it came time for my Trials.

I was finally starting my twelfth year, which meant my ranking and Trials would be the next summer season, and I'd find out if I mattered to my family.

I honestly hoped I wasn't a five. I knew I was strong. The abilities I had were badass, and I didn't need a number to tell me what I could do with them. But I didn't want the attention my brother got. I was the questionable one in the family, the gamble. My Trials could go either way. But my brother grew up in the spotlight. His abilities were so rare that it would have been impossible for him to be anything but a five.

I found myself praying to Pylemo that I'd come out a four. My family wasn't religious, and I'd never admit it to anyone, but I found comfort in the Goddesses.

I was even contemplating only showing one of my abilities during the ranking evaluation just in case by some crazy miracle the Noren family had two rank fives. Everyone knew I possessed illusion, but no one was aware of what else I could do. I never told anyone, not even Sie. I could get a high ranking with my illusion alone—*probably*—which was why I hadn't admitted I had two yet. But I still wasn't sure if I was going to go through with it. The repercussions for me being a three would be far worse than if I was somehow a five.

A muscle in my brother's jaw twitched as he took in our dad. It only lasted a second before he turned to me instead.

"Greyland." Sie smiled, pulling me into a hug.

"I missed you," I murmured into his shoulder because it was the fucking truth. I loved my brother, and I wasn't blind. I knew what he suffered through our whole lives—what he tried so desperately to shelter me from—and one of those things happened to be standing right next to us.

Our father cleared his throat, his only warning to stop showing affection in public. I quickly pulled away from my brother.

"Father," Sie drawled in his best bored-manner expression. I loved that he could mask his emotions because it pissed our dad off to no end. "I thought we agreed to not see each other."

"You know your mother. Once she found out you were staying here, she insisted on having you over for dinner."

"We can't." His fist clenched, then relaxed at his side. "We have to check into the inn and be up early tomorrow. Tell her I'm sorry."

"I'm afraid I won't be doing that. I took the liberty of canceling your rooms. You will be staying with us."

"Rooms... as in plural? Are you planning on hosting all of us at your estate tonight?" Sie asked as he gestured to the group surrounding him, and that's when I noticed her—Sie's fiancée. She was beautiful with long brown hair and bright blue eyes. The contrast was striking.

"I don't think mother would appreciate so many Advenians in her home," Sie added.

"No. Just you and your betrothed," he replied with a lazy grin. "And where is my future daughter-in-law?"

My brother's expression faltered as he looked over at her before gesturing her forward.

"Hello, sir. It's a pleasure to meet you," she said, unable to hide the slight shakiness to her voice.

She gave a subtle bow before extending her hand out to him. I knew he wasn't about to oblige her, and his grunt the next second was confirmation.

"Well, she's pretty for a nix. At least she won't be horrible to bed," was all he said, not even turning to look at her.

Well fuck, I knew my dad was a dick, but I thought he'd try to show a little more respect seeing as she was going to be our future queen, and regardless of that, my brother clearly liked her. The fact that he was so bothered was proof alone. Sie rarely broke for anyone. I'd seen him react less to getting the shit beaten out of him, but the way he was fuming right now...

I stepped in front of our dad—completely aware I'd get yelled at for the move later—but Sie's jaw was set, and his fists were clenched at his sides, and I was more concerned about him doing something stupid.

I reached for his fiancée's still outstretched hand and shook it myself, surprised they were more callused than my own. "It's a pleasure to meet you, *princess*." I hoped the title would remind him of her status and to at least try to be civilized.

"Just Scottie, please," she said, a warm smile melting her stunned expression.

My father clicked his tongue, and as much as I loved that she didn't care about her future title, my father hated it more.

"Greyland." I returned the smile. "Sie's my older brother."

Our dad didn't wait for her to reply as he stalked off toward one of our cars. I followed him as my brother most likely was informing the guards. I figured he'd need a moment to warn the poor girl what she was about to walk in on.

Welcome to the family, Scottie. It's a shit show, and my father will think you're worthless even if you had all the powers in the world, but wait, you're a zero? Yeah, you're totally and royally fucked.

I felt for my brother because tonight was about to be horrendous.

———

THE DRIVE back to our home was long. My brother's fiancée—Scottie—kept looking out the window. Her hands were folded into one another and pressed tightly against her lap.

For as much as Scottie kept looking out the window during the drive, my brother kept looking at *her*. I couldn't help my smile. It was actually nice seeing Sie show any semblance of affection to anyone other than me or Peter.

But my brother's dazed-stupor would be instantly wiped off his face as soon as the necklace she was wearing sparkled against the sun. It honestly looked gaudy, and I had no idea why it was bothering Sie so much, but I wasn't about to ask.

They were both on edge, and despite the fact that anyone would be going into a Noren family dinner, it seemed like there was tension between them aside from the situation they were forced into. Maybe it was just the way she sat ramrod straight, or the way her own gaze flicked briefly toward my brother's. I couldn't understand the expression—not that I was some expert. I sucked when it came to all that crap. I knew how to get laid, but a relationship was foreign to me, and I planned on keeping it that way.

We veered onto the next road with our signature large fence blocking most of the view of the property. I hated the ornate silver trim that was etched and designed into each panel, but I knew Sie hated it even more.

The driver spoke into the scanner box, breaking the silence for the first time. This had to go down in history as the most awkward drive I'd ever taken—and that counted all the times my mom made me take Peter's little sister to school.

Immediately, the doors to the gates groaned open, and I had to mentally prepare myself for the shit show. We were ushered inside the main entrance, and yup, step one of my dad's plan was working. My brother's fiancée was pulling at the sleeves of her dress, trying to hide her zero brand from view as all the Noren servants were lined up in front of us.

"Sie, my darling," Mom's voice sounded as her heels clicked down the hall. She put on a fake smile, but I saw through it, I always did. Sympathy and guilt were fighting for the top place of my emotions any time I looked at her. I hated that she was getting thinner, that she wasn't eating as much as she used to. Her dark eyes were hollow, almost sunken into her head. She was beautiful—and she always would be—but the stress of everything happening was taking a physical toll on her.

"Mother, this is Scotlind Rumor, my fiancée," Sie said as he pulled out of her grip.

Scottie gave another awkward bow. "It's wonderful to finally meet you. Your house is marvelous. Thank you for having us, Mrs. Noren."

My mom smiled, but it didn't reach her eyes. "Oh, this is nothing. But come, the servants are putting dinner on the table. Let's eat while it's still hot."

I followed Sie into the dining room. The place was freaking blazing with the fireplaces roaring to life. I shrugged out of my jacket before slumping into my assigned seat.

My brother sat across from me, next to Scottie, while my parents took their usual spots at the head of the table. I had no appetite tonight for the copious amount of food that was on display, but I forced myself to take a helping. I would miss the servants' cooking when I was at school. If I could eat at home without my dad's looming presence I'd be happy. The food was always delicious, but he tended to ruin the taste for me.

I smirked as my brother served his fiancée first. It was so rare to see him doting on someone.

"Did they not teach you how to properly eat, girl?" Dad asked, eyeing her like a hawk. I took one glance and saw she was using the wrong utensil—not that they made it easy for her by lining up every single one we owned. "Tell me about your upbringing, Scotlind. What of your parents?"

"My family passed away when I was seven years old. LakeWood has always been my home."

"Hmm, an orphan," Dad scoffed, but he already knew everything about her. After she was announced, he went crazy and started digging into her past. It honestly felt more like an obsession. "Interesting how you, with no power, were the only one to survive. A fire, wasn't it?"

Scottie looked up from her plate, her bright blue eyes widened, but she didn't say anything.

"Were your family nixes as well?"

"Maverich," Mom interjected, her voice lowering.

"What, Katherine? I'm just trying to get to know the girl better. After all, she is going to join our family." He shoved a piece of meat into his mouth. "I was told that you were trying out to be a guard before you were selected for my son."

"Yes, I was," she replied softly.

"You believed that was possible? Achievable, I mean, for someone like you?" My father's voice was calm, which was always when he was at his scariest. "You didn't consider being a servant?"

Sie slammed his fist onto the table, rattling the dishes, and Dad smiled up at him before adding, "You see, that's the problem with this arrangement. Rank zeroes should never be queen. You shouldn't have to marry my son. It's very unfair to you, Scotlind, that they are giving you a job you are incapable of succeeding in. Our High Council owes it to our society to place our people fairly among their rankings. It's the reason the Trials were established. They truly did you and Sie a disservice."

Well shit.

My brother's fists clenched the armrest of the seat so hard I swore he was going to break it. "That's enough," he gritted.

"It's not too late," Dad went on, completely ignoring him. "Sie, you can help her by renouncing this marriage. You should marry someone of a high rank. Someone who is fitting of your status. Think of your future children. If you reproduce with her"—he gestured toward Scottie who was frozen in her seat—"your kids will be weak. Her blood will taint their power. It's a waste of your rank five. I'll make you both a very generous deal," he said with a smile. "Son, if you agree to marry Reagan, I will welcome Miss Rumor here with open arms at our estate."

I shifted in my seat. I knew he was going to pull something like this, but I never imagined he'd be so blunt about it. I was staring at Scotlind when her eyes drifted to mine. I attempted to give her a smile, but honestly this dinner was far past pleasantries.

"Scotlind will not be a servant here," Sie growled. His chair groaned against the floor as he pushed it back and stood. "She will be my wife, and you will show her respect as your future queen." He pulled her up by the arm, lifting—more like dragging—her out of her seat. "Come on, let's go."

———

Mom and I were forced to finish our dinner, even though we would have stayed anyway. It was our unspoken agreement—since Dad never stayed a second longer than it took him to finish his meal, we did. It was one of the few times it was just the two of us. We just had to make it through *him* finishing his meal first.

No one talked after Sie and Scottie left. I tried to not openly glare at my dad as he glowered after them.

I looked up at Mom, wondering if she knew Dad was going to say all of that. Her dark eyes met mine and softened the moment it was just the two of us. She tried to smile, but lately she couldn't even pretend anymore.

"You need to eat, Mom," I said softly. She'd only been twirling the food around her plate with her fork.

She sighed. "Don't worry about me, Grey."

"But I do worry about you. I'm leaving tomorrow morning, and you're going to be alone with him."

She tried to smile again, her lips moving a fraction of an inch as she leaned over the table and patted my dark hair. It was jet black, just like hers and my brother's, but Sie's waves resembled more of her curls, while mine just looked like I didn't brush it, which I never did, so I guess it was my own fault.

"I'm fine, Grey." She sighed as she sank back into her seat and pushed her untouched plate away. "By the way, I talked with the Fervics, you're taking Lilia to school tomorrow."

My fork clattered as I dropped it onto the table. "What?"

"You're driving Lilia to school when you leave tomorrow."

My teeth ground together. "Mom, I'm not driving her to school."

Her eyes widened. "Why not? I thought you two got along?"

I scoffed. "Just because Peter Fervic is Sie's best friend, doesn't automatically make Lilia mine."

"Well, either way, you're taking her to school. You know her parents can't afford the public transportation fees."

Yeah, cause the Fervics were the complete opposite of the Norens. They came from a family of low ranks. It was honestly a shock when Peter's shapeshifting powers manifested. He was the only strong Advenian out of them, and Lilia, well, she got the shit end of the ability gene pool because everyone knew she didn't have any. Well, everyone knew except Lilia herself—the girl was in denial that she was going to be a zero.

"I thought Dad didn't like our association with the Fervics," I said, trying another tactic, because the idea of spending the hour-long drive with her sounded worse than our dinner tonight. "Won't he be pissed once he finds out I drove her?"

Appearances were everything to my dad, and I knew my mom wouldn't hear the end of it.

She narrowed her eyes. "Leave your father to me. Besides, their name should rise in status soon once Peter takes over as Sie's second."

Another thing my dad was pissed about—he hated my brother's friendship with Peter, and besides the fact that Peter was insanely powerful, the name he came from wasn't.

It didn't matter how high up her brother climbed, Lilia was going to be left behind.

Unless my brother's new fiancée changed things. Maybe Tennebris was on the cusp of reworking their opinions on the ranking system...

Maybe being declared a rank zero wouldn't be so detrimental if our future queen was one.

Maybe.

TWO
LILIA

"Go back to bed, Peter," I groaned, turning over on my cot.

I hated mornings, and I especially hated this morning. I didn't want my brother to leave. Our home felt empty ever since he went to Palm with Sie, and having him back for one night wasn't nearly enough.

"That's no way to treat your favorite brother."

I knew he was smiling without having to turn over and look.

"You're my only brother." I rolled my eyes.

The cot shifted as Peter stood and started walking toward the window...

"No—" I half shrieked as he pulled our only blind open, and the Tennebrisian sun streamed through the window. I slammed my pillow over my head, trying to block out the brightness, but Peter ripped it from me.

"You're cruel and—"

"You love me," he cut me off as I finally sat up before leaning my back against the wall. We shared a bedroom—and regardless of the fact that it was way too small and only had enough room for our two cots with a narrowed walkway between them—I loved it.

"You're lucky I do." I found myself grinning back before he

chucked the pillow at me. I tucked it under my arms, leaning forward as I sat cross-legged on the mattress. "Do you have to go?"

"Yeah." He frowned. "The monorail is leaving, and we still have to finish our tour."

I pouted. "Well, give me a hug so I can go back to bed."

"Lilia, didn't Mum tell you?"

"Tell me what?"

"You're coming with me."

I perked up. "Really? I'm going on the tour with you?" I couldn't keep the excitement from my voice. Peter told me all about Scotlind Rumor last night, and the idea of meeting her now had me fully awake. I prayed she was the change we needed. If a rank zero could be queen, it meant there was hope for the rest of us. It meant there was a chance we could be other things too.

My mind was whirling last night, thinking about my course load going into my twelfth and final year. Maybe I could really Trial for what I wanted—

"Not on the tour, but you're coming with me to go to the Norens."

"Why?" I stilled as my heart started to beat erratically.

"Grey is taking you to school." Peter tousled his shaggy blonde hair as his green eyes met mine. I was always envious of the coloring growing up. Actually, I was envious of everything about Peter—while my eyes were a mix between brown and gold with only a smidge of green—his were wholly green. Everything about him was better and brighter. Even his hair had more volume to it while mine was dull and flat. It was so straight that even if I kept it in tight braids, it wouldn't hold a curl. Most days it wouldn't even hold the braids.

"School doesn't start for another week—"

"I know, but Mum arranged for him to take you, and he's leaving today."

"But—" I started, but he cut me off.

"Lil, you need to go with him. It'll help Mum."

"I know, I know." I hated that it was true. It would cost my parents a fortune to pay the transportation fee to take me to school.

Each village only had one school, and ours happened to be located by the coast. Kitlarn was the largest out of the six, and because of it, everything was spread out. I hated that we weren't from LakeWood or Narway, where everything was within walking distance from the town. So if riding with Greyland made things easier for my parents, I'd do it.

I wasn't even supposed to be here. It was only ever supposed to be Peter. They only wanted one kid—not that they would ever admit it to my face—but I knew the burden I gave them. They didn't think the past Lakimi would be so successful. They never imagined having two mouths to feed. They couldn't afford it.

"When do we have to leave?"

"Now."

"What?" I bolted out of bed. "And you're only waking me up *now*?"

Peter shrugged. "It's not like it's going to take you a while to pack."

My eyes narrowed. "It would have been nice to take a bath first," I snapped as I started throwing my clothes into a bag. He was right. It didn't take me long. I didn't own much and was thankful that Kitlarn had uniforms because everyone would have known I was repeating the same outfits if they didn't.

"Take one when you get to the dorms that way you aren't wasting Mum and Dad's water."

I knew he was right. It was one of the perks to the dorms, free running water, even if only the upper class had access to heat. But now I was going to have to sit in Greyland's car looking and smelling like this…

I internally groaned before following Peter out onto the drive, because there was nothing I could do about it.

———

I THOUGHT the only thing that could make this morning worse was the fact that I just missed Sie and Scotlind, but then I saw Greyland glaring at me in his foyer, and I knew *he* was definitely the worst part about today.

Mrs. Noren was standing next to him, a sweet smile on her face. I honestly had no idea how she was so nice when her husband was a jerk and her two sons had anger problems.

"Hi, Lilia," she said. "How is your mother?"

"She's good," I responded, shifting my pack onto my other shoulder. Our mothers became friends at the same time Peter and Sie did, although they only saw each other whenever Grey's dad was out of town.

Greyland's jaw was ticking as he ground it from side to side. "Let's go," he drawled as he stormed past me, leaving his four bags on the floor of the foyer.

I gave Mrs. Noren a wave goodbye before I reluctantly followed her son out onto their driveway. Several servants trailed behind me and loaded up his car in complete silence. He didn't even say goodbye to his own mother or acknowledge any of the servants.

I waited until his bags were loaded before I sucked in a breath and forced myself to sit down in the passenger seat. Greyland was already in the car, waiting as the gate barricading his home groaned open. His hands were white knuckled on the wheel as he stared blankly ahead. I threw my own pack between my legs, closed the door, and planted my hands against my thighs.

I could do this.

Once the gate fully opened, my head slammed into the seat rest as he gunned the pedal. I was always fascinated with cars. I knew they were powered by electric users from Lux, same as the monorail. It was why they were so rare and hard to come by. The Norens were the only reason I even knew what a singular vehicle looked like.

Only the wealthy could afford the astronomical fees it would cost to send an electric user from Lux here by a work visa. But of course all four of them had their own car, and not just any car, a luxurious one. The public transportation that took everyone else to school were battered down vans. Their seats had permanent stains and the cloth material was peeling at the edges.

But Greyland's car was all cream leather and flashing gadgets. I couldn't even begin to comprehend how it all worked. Air and fire users must have put something into the seats because warm or cool air escaped through tiny holes depending on which setting you chose.

It was a ridiculous show of their wealth, and I hated it.

At least when I was younger, I had the option to ride with Peter and Sie. The latter liked to leave at the last possible second for school. I wasn't sure if it was by his own choice or if his father forced him to stay.

Only Grey liked to go early.

I exhaled a deep breath and prepared myself for the butterflies in my stomach as Greyland sped through the winding roads.

He was in a foul mood, even worse than his normal closed-off-asshole-vibes. Neither of us talked, and as much as I wanted to know how meeting Scotlind Rumor went last night, I wasn't about to ask. Besides, I probably didn't want to know what *he* thought. Grey and his friends made it abundantly clear how they felt about rank zeroes.

I internally groaned, hating that I had to go through another school year with them. I didn't think it was possible for Greyland and his friends to make my life any worse than it already was, but I also said the same thing every year, and somehow they always surpassed what they did before.

My stomach was in knots just thinking about them. This was our final year before Trials, and if I knew his friends, they would make the Goddesses cry if they could.

Which meant they one thousand percent were going to try to make me cry.

I was in for a terrible twelfth year.

THREE
GREYLAND

"Noren, wait up."

I looked over my shoulder to see Mack and Lander running toward me. Well, Mack was running, Lander was walking with his hands in his pocket.

"Hey," I called as Mack reached me. "I thought you guys weren't coming until the start of term?" They never came early, which was one of the reasons I did.

"Mack said he saw you," Lander drawled, ignoring my question. "I thought differently."

Mack grinned at me. "I told Lander I saw you driving Lilia Fervic. He didn't believe me."

Here it goes.

I had already dropped my bags off in my dorm—which I was sharing with Lander this year because Mack got Colton. The four of us had been rotating every year since we were little, and it was just my luck that my last year here, I was stuck with Lander. I saw his bags and decided to go for a walk, having no desire to interact with him any earlier than I had to.

I was only friends with Lander for show. Neither of us liked each other anymore, at least not since fifth year when he became interested in girls and didn't like it when some of them preferred me instead. Now everything was a hidden competition, and if we hadn't been friends since childhood, neither of us would have even bothered with keeping it up.

"My mom thought it would be a good idea since her brother is going to be Sie's second." I shrugged. "I drove her for appearances only."

"Your mother is delusional if she thinks having the Fervic girl around you will do any good," Lander barked a laugh. "Her brother is a different story, but she's nothing more than a nix no matter what happens to Peter."

"Right, well, it wasn't my choice. I couldn't drive here fast enough."

Mack chuckled. "She's not bad to look at. It couldn't have been *that* bad."

Lander and I both glared at him.

"What?" He shrugged. "I'm serious. Regardless of the fact that she's going to be a zero, you have to admit, she's a little attractive. Besides, you could have had to drive her friend, Grace, who doesn't know when to shut up. At least Lilia is quiet."

Quiet wasn't an adjective I'd use to describe Lilia, but I wasn't about to correct him. She was reserved and knew when to hold her tongue, but that didn't mean she always did.

Lander smirked. "You're right, Mack. At least little Fervic would be a good fuck, but I actually think Grace is better." He put his hand over my shoulder and squeezed. "I like that she doesn't know how to shut up. It could be a fun challenge to teach her. Get her to fill that big mouth with—"

"Why are you guys here early?" I interrupted, drawing the conversation away from Lilia and her friend. "I thought you weren't coming for another week."

I did it to myself. The first time Lander talked his usual shit about Lilia, I should have stopped him. But I didn't, and now it was too late to start. I let my friends be a dick to her because... well I wasn't even sure why. Maybe I was pushing her away on purpose, maybe I was scared of what would happen if I let her in. Not that it mattered. She hated me, and even if she didn't, I could never be with her.

Even though Tennebrisians were allowed to marry for love, I wasn't. I knew my father wouldn't allow me to end up with anyone of a lower rank, especially not a zero.

I didn't have to listen to him. Technically, after my Trials, I could be free of my father. But every time I imagined screwing him over, I thought of Mom. If I purposely turned down an order—after the Trials or not—she would suffer the consequences. Sie didn't see it that way. He wasn't close to her like I was. He couldn't be. Our dad never let him. But while Dad put all his focus into Sie, Mom did the same for me.

I got the better end of the deal. Mom was gentle, loving, kind. Literally everything our dad wasn't. The only fault I could say about her was that she didn't have a backbone. She didn't know how to stand up against him, and her defense mechanism was self-deprivation and closing herself off.

Sie thought she was cold and heartless because of it. She never stepped in when Dad beat me, but Sie did. He always protected me from the brunt of Dad's rage. It was why they didn't get along—Sie thought it should have been *her* stepping in. But I knew she couldn't. It was her own way of protecting herself. I could see that, could look past it. Sie couldn't.

Maybe it was messed up because sometimes I felt like the parent, like I needed to be the responsible one and protect her. I couldn't stomach marrying someone Dad picked out for me just as much as I couldn't handle my mother taking the hit for it if I didn't.

Once I graduated from Kitlarn, I planned to move out of the house as soon as possible. It was one of the many reasons I was following in Sie's footsteps and decided to Trial for a guard. On top of the fact that guards were encouraged *not* to take a spouse—which meant no Goddess-damned awful arranged marriage—I wanted to be as far away from Dad as possible. Most guards ended up in Palm, and if being one gave me the chance at living away from him, I was going to take it.

"I came early because Lander did." Mack shrugged.

I turned to Lander.

"Tell me about last night," he said, avoiding my question *again*.

"What about it?"

"I heard your brother and Scotlind Rumor were at your house for the tour."

"Yeah."

"Well, is she hot?"

"I'm not talking about my brother's future wife like that."

"That means yes." Lander grinned, and I had the urge to punch him in his too-white smile. "How did Daddy Noren take it?"

I gave him a look. I hated the nickname my friends had for him, but I knew they only said it to piss me off. "How do you think? She's a zero."

"Your dad is a badass," Mack chimed in.

More like just an ass, but I wasn't about to correct him. No one knew he used to beat the living shit out of my brother—it was a perk that Sie was always training because any bruise he got was written off as just that.

It was the only thing Peter and Lilia had that I was envious of— both of their parents were nice. I still remember the first time Peter invited Sie and I over to their house for dinner. The food was bland— they couldn't even afford bread, which I was pretty sure was why Peter always ate a boatload of it whenever he came to our house. But even with only eating weeks old dried meat, it was nicer than our dinners. They actually talked, and it wasn't just lectures and criticism, but deep, real conversations. I almost choked on my food when their dad pulled their mom in for a hug and kissed her in front of everyone. I'd never seen it before. Openly expressing love and affection was foreign to us.

"I'm surprised your brother didn't put up a fight," Lander said. "The Council is out of their minds for giving him a zero."

Giving him like Scotlind was property he now owned. "Yeah," I half-heartedly agreed, not having the energy for this conversation anymore. I wasn't going to tell them my brother was obsessed with the girl and that being engaged to her was probably the first time I ever saw Sie excited about something. "I'm going to the dining hall."

I started making my way toward the hub of campus. Everything of importance was located by the ocean—the dining hall, the classrooms, the auditorium. I would have returned to school even sooner if I could, but today was the first official day of the new school year. They closed everything down for the four week break between years.

Now Kitlarn students had a week to trickle in before classes started, and I found myself only liking the school when it was empty.

"Great. We'll come with you." Lander grinned. "I can always eat."

And I knew this was going to be a long year.

FOUR
LILIA

"Hey, Lil."

Lil, not *Little*—it was how I knew this wasn't real.

It was Greyland, but wasn't. The dream version I concocted of him always came to me in my sleep.

I hated it.

But I couldn't stop it.

It wasn't like any of this would actually happen. It never could. Reality check: Greyland Noren was the biggest jerk I'd ever met—but in my dreams—he was sweet, caring, *nice*. He was everything I wanted him to be.

"Hi, Grey." I smiled. The dream always started the same. Everything else faded away until it was only him. The world around my vision was gray—probably my subconscious channeling his name. He started walking toward me and slowly things materialized around us as he came into focus.

I'd been dreaming of him for a while, ever since ninth year. I told myself before bed that I wouldn't, but every night he'd find his way into my mind.

I thanked Pylemo none of his friends possessed mind reading abilities because if anyone knew what I dreamt of—what we did at night—I'd die from embarrassment.

"Are you ready for twelfth year?"

I sat down on the sofa that appeared as he took the seat next to me. It was our most common setting in my dreams—a green couch. "As ready as I'll ever be. You?" I tucked my legs under me.

"Same." His expression was somber, and I knew his thoughts had drifted. It was strange, in my dreams he was complex, had his own way of thinking. Probably because I didn't think he was capable of anything more than snide remarks and getting drunk with his friends in real life.

A blanket appeared, and he draped it over my shoulders, then used the movement to curl into my side—just slightly. It was only enough for his thigh to touch mine, but neither of us pulled away.

"I wish you were like this in real life," I said after a while. Sometimes we would talk. Sometimes we just sat in silence. But it was never awkward—*because it wasn't real, Lilia.*

His dark eyes soaked me in, but he didn't comment. He looked exactly the same outside of my dreams. Black eyes, short dark hair to match. His complexion was pale like all the Norens were. But he was broader than he was before. He now had muscles filling his lithe body. My dream version of him changed as he did in real life, and I knew it was because I was attracted to him, although I'd never admit it to anyone.

The only thing about him that wasn't the same was his personality.

I hated myself for this, for still wanting him even though he was a complete dick. But I had convinced myself somewhere in year ten that I only liked the idea of him.

I didn't actually like *him.*

———

I AWOKE with a start and realized Grace had thrown a pillow at my face.

"Get up, or we're going to be late."

I groaned, pushing the pillow off my dorm bed and looked at the clock—Kitlarn Academy favored electricity more than the other five schools in Tennebris with Palm and Addler following closely behind. It was only LakeWood, Narway, and Backerly that tried to limit it. All the electricity in Backerly went into the AASP for the space program—which left the school with nothing—and Narway and LakeWood were so poor compared to the rest of the Dark Kingdom that it wasn't a surprise they couldn't afford it.

Kitlarn only had two buildings for their dorms. It wasn't divided by gender or potential ranks but by wealth.

The building I was in—Jelckin Hall—was for the lower class, for the families who paid the bare minimum to have their children go to school. The building Grey and his friends slept in was designated for the rich. In order to stay there, your parents had to contribute and donate to the school. I'd never been in Hiwet Hall before, but I'd heard stories in class about it.

Compared to my childhood home—which we were lucky to have candles burning and definitely didn't own anything with electricity—I loved our dorm and was completely content in Jelckin Hall.

For starters, it was the only place on campus I could be free of Greyland and his friends. And it still had everything I needed. I didn't mind the communal bathhouse, and I liked sharing a room with Grace. From years of sleeping in the same room as Peter, I was used to cramped spaces and always having company, and that's how I liked it. I hated being alone.

Technically, Grace should be staying in Hiwet Hall. Her family was crazy rich, and she even offered to make contributions on my behalf so we could sleep there together, but I refused. So being the amazing friend that she was, she gave up the luxury of Hiwet to be with me.

Supposedly, Hiwet Hall was divided into dorm suites. Each space had a shared living area with two private rooms spanning from there. And they didn't have to use communal bathhouses like Jelckin. Each suite had their own, so you only had to share with one other person.

"Grace, it's five in the morning. Classes don't start for another two hours."

"I know, but I want to get there early. Scope out our seats."

I hated that everyone in my life—which was only my two friends and my brother—were morning people. I wasn't. Despite how much I slept, I felt chronically tired. Sometimes I swore I was even more tired when I woke up than when I went to bed.

But there was another added perk to campus that I didn't have in my family home—tea. The caffeine was the only reason I survived school. It was what had me eventually rolling out of bed every morning.

The week went by too fast. I actually didn't mind coming to school early—despite the fact that I had to drive with Greyland, but I hadn't seen him since, so I counted it as a win.

I took the opportunity to bathe every day and go to the library to read about mending. It was my dream, what I wanted to do more than anything, and if I had some sort of ability, I would have been allowed to.

Tennebrisian menders were assistants to the Luxian healers that were stationed through a work visa. We didn't possess the ability to heal with our hands, but I actually liked the idea of doing it old school. I liked wrapping wounds and trying to figure out what concoctions could rapidly accelerate healing. It was addicting to see tangible results without abilities. I found it therapeutic.

My second favorite thing to do was cook. Which was a more reasonable Trial for me to go into. It was technically above being a servant—which most rank zeroes were—but I was good enough that I still stood a chance. But Trialing for a mender... I'd been told I was delusional way too many times by my parents—in the nicest way they could possibly put it. I got it. I understood it. They just didn't want to see me get hurt. And if I failed my Trial in mending, it meant a one way ticket into being a servant.

Grace could Trial in anything she wanted. I was envious of that. She liked mending too. It was how we became friends during year two, and we've been inseparable ever since. Jaxson came into our duo five years later.

Another pillow was thrown at my face courtesy of Grace. Her

energy was eerily similar to Peter. "If you don't get up in the next thirty seconds, I'm leaving without you."

"Okay, okay. I'm up." I chucked the pillow back at her, which she stopped midair before sending it flying onto her bed. Then she tucked her sheets into the corners all while standing in the middle of our room.

I was jealous of her power, but I'd never tell her that. When we first realized I most likely wasn't going to manifest any abilities, she didn't use her telekinesis for six months before I realized what she was doing. I yelled at her and since then demanded she didn't act differently toward me. Just because I had no powers—*that I knew of*—didn't mean she couldn't use hers around me.

I grabbed my towel and a pair of bath shoes that Grace gave me and headed to the communal bathhouse down the hall.

I was back and dressed ten minutes later. Grace was already ready to go. She had her golden hair tied into a tight bun, and her brand new school uniform was pressed to perfection.

I decided to let my hair down. It didn't matter how I styled it, it usually fell out of whatever hold I attempted to put it into.

"Come on, Jaxs is meeting us for breakfast."

I swore Grace would have woken me up earlier if the dining hall opened sooner, but it started at five-thirty on the dot, and no amount of pillows could get me out of bed without the promise of tea.

It was a five minute walk to the hub of campus, and I embraced the morning breeze as we walked along the path separating the ocean from the campus. Kitlarn Academy was the closest Tennebrisian town toward the shield, and my parents could only afford two school uniforms, which meant the navy coat to match wasn't an option. If it wasn't for Grace giving me one, I never would have survived. She claimed it was one of her old ones, but I knew she bought it new for me. I was five inches taller than her and it somehow fit me perfectly.

Jaxson was already waiting for us as the doors opened to the dining hall.

"Hey, Grace. Hey, Lilia," he said as Grace pulled him in for a hug.

"Hi, Jaxs." I smiled once he finally stepped out of Grace's grip. The three of us were the only ones in the hall. Most students didn't start to dwindle in for another thirty minutes. And as much as I loved to sleep and hated waking up early, I couldn't deny that it was an added perk to have the dining hall to ourselves.

I was nervous about school this year. Peter had warned me that more eyes might be on Greyland and I because of everything happening with them. It was our first time back at school since Sie was declared the prince, and even though Greyland always grew up in the spotlight as a Noren, I never did. Peter was popular when he attended school, and everyone knew we were siblings, but no one really cared about me before. But now that he was declared Sie's future second, I was terrified things were going to be different.

I hated attention, and I hated the heated glares. Mainly because everyone that looked at me always compared me to Peter—he was everything I wasn't, and no matter how hard I tried to brush it off, I was the disappointment. I could feel everyone's resentment—*my parents shouldn't have had me.* Even if my parents didn't feel that way, it's what everyone else saw when they looked at me.

"Soooo, I have something I have to admit," Grace drawled as we slowly started to fill our trays with food. I grabbed an apple and a piece of toast before I made it to the drink station. I poured earl grey into the biggest cup the dining hall had. I opted for plain tea in the morning and usually drank two or three sweeter ones by the afternoon.

"What did you do now?" Jaxson teased as he nudged her. His hair was buzzed now, exposing his dark skin through the short layer. Last time I saw him, his curls were long. I knew Jaxson liked to cut it every so often—complaining that his hair got in his eyes—but I still hated it whenever he did. I always wanted curly hair, and his curls were picture perfect spirals that made it feel like a sin whenever he got rid of them.

"You know how I offered to hand in your elective schedule, Lilia?"

"Yeah..." I said, taking a sip of my tea, wincing as it burned the tip of my tongue.

"Well I couldn't help but notice how you picked cooking classes as your electives." Dread started to fill me as my mind raced through possible scenarios of what she was going to say next. All students in twelfth year had certain requirements they had to meet. We had set classes that we all took together, but the closer you got to graduation, the more freedom you had to fill in the gaps of your schedule. It was meant to allow us to pick classes that would help prepare us for what we wanted to Trial in.

"I know you think you won't pass if you Trial in mending, but I wanted you to have the option," Grace continued as we found our usual table near the bayside window.

"Grace, what did you do?"

"Well, I checked and cooking and mending electives aren't at the same time, and I made sure it worked with your entire schedule, which it does by the way—"

"Grace Marie Kilena, *what did you do?*" I asked again, this time raising my voice. My best friend could ramble. She was known for always blabbing, and I needed her to get to the point *now*, even though I was fairly certain I already knew where this conversation was heading.

"I sort of signed you up for both."

"You WHAT?"

"I just want you to have the option to change your mind, and you need a certain amount of credits in mending in order to qualify for Trialing in it. I added it up. We've always taken the same amount of classes and you would have been short."

"I know I was short, Grace. I'm not Trialing in mending. My mind is made up."

"But I don't think it should be."

I set my tea down. Most days I opted for delusion. I hoped and prayed that I had some ability that just wasn't overtly strong, and I wouldn't notice until I had my ranking evaluation. Maybe I had low level knowledge absorption. I usually didn't have to study as much as my friends, and Grace always teased me about it when I'd explain our study material to Jaxson for the fifth time and he still couldn't grasp it. But I also knew the reality of my situation. Even though my parents were both ones, and my brother was a four, our family came from a long line of zeroes, and deep down, I knew I was going to be one too.

"What if things change, Lilia?" she continued, re-pinning a golden piece of hair that fell out of her bun. My hair was pale white while hers was vibrant and sun-kissed. "With Sie marrying a rank zero, things could be different. She's going to be the queen. Do you realize how huge this is for people like you?"

People like me. Everyone else in Kitlarn was confident I was a zero. But Grace's words... I wanted it too much. I wanted things to change, and I prayed to Pylemo that Scotlind Rumor would be that for me.

"I just want you to have options," she continued. "Sie will become king before we finish our twelfth year, and you never know what could happen—"

"Thank you, Grace," I cut her off.

"So does that mean you're gonna do it?" She hadn't touched her breakfast yet, which was a pastry loaded with extra sugary toppings. Anything sweet, regardless of the time of day, Grace was consuming it.

"I can't exactly change it now," I said, picking my tea back up. "Our schedules were due two days ago."

"Great." She started housing her pastry now. "Because mending electives are a lot, and your schedule is packed."

I held my free hand out. "Can I have it?"

Every time I asked her for my copy of my schedule, she had made some lame excuse for not handing it over—she forgot it, then she couldn't find it, one time it was "she needed to eat first before she could think about anything school related." She even resorted to pretending to be asleep once. I should have seen through it. She was the lightest sleeper I'd ever met in my life. Me, on the other hand, when I was out, I was out. Nothing could wake me up, which was why my friend and my brother found that throwing things at me was most effective.

Grace reluctantly handed it over, and I groaned as I finally scanned the paper schedule that would be my life for the next year. Grace wasn't joking about my schedule being full. I could say goodbye to sleeping in… permanently. My first class started at seven, and my last one didn't end until dinner time.

"Why do I have to wake up early on the weekend?" I gasped.

"Um." Grace bit her lip. "In order to Trial in mending, on top of taking the elective classes, you need volunteer work. Experience in the specialty—" My stomach dropped as she finished her sentence. "—so you and I are the menders for this year's Guard Class, which means we're going to travel for the Six Battles."

The Six Battles—the competitor team for the Guard—the team Greyland and his friends were going to be on. They were the best fighters in our class.

So much for avoiding him this year…

FIVE
GREYLAND

Everyone was forced to take Ability Class. It was the one mandated time we had to practice our powers. Even if you had none, you had to attend.

The only ability that wasn't practiced during the class was compulsion. Luckily, Lander *mostly* followed the rules. I knew he abused his ability when he wasn't at school, though, and I had no idea why I was relieved Kitlarn had the rule. It wasn't like he could use it on me—only my brother could compel another ranked Tennebrisian.

But if I was being honest with myself, I knew why I wanted compulsion banned, and the reason had pale blonde hair, hazel eyes, and shallow dimples.

The idea of having to watch Lander compel Lilia made me sick to my stomach. I wasn't delusional enough to think she would be able to avoid it her whole life—I knew as soon as we graduated there would be no rules. But at least I wouldn't be around to witness it. The chances of us being assigned to the same place were slim to none, and I'd finally be able to put her out of my mind.

"If you need something to occupy yourself with over the next hour, *Little*, I can give you something to do." Everyone laughed as Colton made a handjob motion in front of Lilia.

"I don't think you've ever had a girl's hand come remotely close to your dick, Colton. You wouldn't know what to do with yourself," Grace snapped back as she pushed Lilia in front of her. Jaxson ground his jaw but didn't comment. The guy was a dweeb, and I had no idea why Lilia was friends with him.

"Give it a try, Grace, and maybe I'll let you find out just how well I can control myself." Even though he'd deny it to his grave, it was obvious Colton liked Lilia's friend. The girl was the shortest in our year, while Colton and I were the tallest. Colton was huge—in every way imaginable, and his afro added an extra inch. If we were fighting without our abilities, it was usually a gamble of who would win.

Grace made a face. "If I did that your friends would have nothing to do."

"Fuck off," I snapped.

It was probably the only thing that Lander and I agreed on—no one brought our names into their mouths. If they did, I made sure it was their last.

If Grace wasn't Lilia's friend, I would have put her in an illusion until she was bawling on the floor for even insinuating that any of us gave Colton a handjob. And if Jaxson had said it, I would have physically beat him until he was crying.

Grace looked at me before practically shoving Lilia again and dragging her toward the other end of the room.

Abilities Class was the only lecture our entire year took together so it was always held in the largest gymnasium Kitlarn had. The space was open with chairs around the perimeter for anyone who couldn't manifest. It was where Lilia always sat. She usually opted to face the bayside and ignore the room wholly. I didn't blame her.

I always found it humiliating that our entire year was forced to take the class. I understood it. You technically didn't know for sure you were a zero until you took your Trial. But there was always a group of students that just watched. It was a waste of their time, and I always felt like I was rubbing my ability in their faces.

I pulled my focus away from Lilia and her friends to wait for our professor to show and separate us into our groups. I was paired with the other illusion users, which was the only thing I liked about the class—it gave me a break from Lander.

There were only seven illusion users in my year, and I was by far the best one. I could always tear their illusions apart. Making them myself, I knew the tell-tale signs to look for. The slight glimmer around the edges of your vision, the fine details that might not be depicted perfectly. Even smells were different if the user couldn't capture it correctly. It was why I was so attentive. The better I knew my surroundings, the more realistic I could warp things.

"Everyone gather around," Professor Jean called as she made her way toward the center of the room. Her copper hair was pulled into a tight ponytail—as it always was. The teachers had a variation of our school uniform to wear, all a mixture of navy blue, pale gray, and white. I unbuttoned my blazer and threw it off to the side before I walked to the middle of the room with everyone else.

"This year things are going to be different. Since this is your last year in Kitlarn, and you'll be taking your Trials at the end of it, we will no longer separate you by your projected abilities. Everyone will participate together. You will be encouraged to use your abilities on each other."

"Even compulsion?" Lander asked as he came up beside me.

Professor Jean's brown eyes narrowed in on him. She honestly was intimidating as hell. I always thought she was an even match for our Guard Professor. The only difference was that nothing got past Professor Jean.

"You know full well compulsion is banned, Mr. Autions. You can use your energy weaponry in my class and that is it." Her gaze left Lander and shifted through the rest of us. "We'll start with two people every class. Since we meet daily, eventually, you will have an opportunity to go up against everyone."

"Greyland and Laci, you're up first." I stepped up to the circle drawn in the middle of the room. "Greyland has illusion, and Laci is a telepath. Let's see what you can do."

I looked at Laci who was staring up at me with pupils nearly blown. Besides Guard Class, we'd never used our abilities on someone else before, especially on someone who didn't have the same power.

"What are we supposed to do?" I asked.

Professor Jean glared at me like I was asking the most idiotic question. "Think of an object in your mind. Laci will use her abilities to find out what the object is. Greyland, you use your illusion to make her find something else. You'll stop when Laci thinks she has it. I have lie detection so I'll know who won."

I rolled my shoulders.

"Greyland, do you have your object?"

For some reason a red apple came to mind. "Yes."

"Okay, start," Professor Jean called.

I'd never used my illusion like this, and the idea thrilled me. My body flared immediately with my markings. Mine were thick bands around my abdomen that luckily were mostly hidden beneath my uniform.

I felt Laci in my head immediately. Growing up with Sie, I learned to recognize the feeling. Anyone that was a mind reader in some capacity had a tell-tale presence to it. Laci's was lighter and fainter than my brothers. I could feel her shifting through my thoughts. I kept my mind blank as I slowly started my illusion. If I wanted it to feel real, I had to learn how she used her abilities first. I needed her to believe that it was still her navigating through me.

She shifted through my mind like water. Flowy, always moving, almost seamless. I used it, finally bringing my powers to imitate hers. When I had her wrapped in an illusion, making her believe she was still in my mind, sifting through my thoughts, I let an image of a pencil slip. I sent a flicker of emotion through too. Just a split second, so fast that she would've missed it if she wasn't paying attention. I had to make her believe I was forcing everything away from the pencil.

"Got it." Laci grinned. I dropped my illusion the moment I felt her leave my head. "Pencil."

"No." I smirked.

Professor Jean stepped between us. "Greyland won this round."

As I walked back toward my friends. I caught a glimpse of Lilia eating an apple.

A red apple.

———

"WHAT THE HELL is *she* doing here?"

I followed Lander's gaze to pale blonde hair. Well there were two blondes—one short and golden and the other taller and paler—and I couldn't tear my gaze away from the latter.

"This is a joke, right?" Colton asked as he looked up too. He arrived in Kitlarn Academy last night, just in time for our first day of classes, while I'd been stuck with Lander and Mack all week.

Beside Ability Class, everything was an introduction to the year, and the day dragged. They always had Guard Class last—mostly because, if you got injured, they didn't want you to miss out on any of the other lectures. And people got injured a lot.

"She can't seriously be Trialing to be a mender?" Colton added as he pulled his afro into a high bun. "She's a nix."

We all changed prior to stepping onto the mats. I hated our white uniform. I was so pale it washed me out, but Colton made it look good. The color contrasted against his dark skin.

Lander smiled as he dropped his bags down onto the mats. "This year just got a whole lot more fun." He ran his fingers through his thick brown hair as he openly stared at Lilia and her friend. "Maybe I'll actually let you beat me up a little bit, Noren, if it means getting *tended* to."

"If I beat the shit out of you, it's because I'm the better fighter," I snapped. "Not because you *let* me."

He finally turned his gaze away from them to look at me. He still had a smile on his face. "If that's what you want to tell yourself."

My eyes narrowed. Yeah, I was definitely punching him when we fought today. Lander and I were the best fighters in Kitlarn when we used our abilities. I only fought with my illusion, but I'd been practicing and honing it so much that it came effortlessly. I knew I was good.

Lander had compulsion, which he couldn't use against me since I was ranked, but his energy weaponry had landed me with the menders more times than I could count. It wasn't that he was a better fighter, but it was hard to not get sliced open when he could use weapons, and I couldn't.

Mack and Colton were both good too. Colton had telekinesis and knowledge absorption and was the strongest physically out of all of us. When it came to fighting without abilities, he had almost everyone beat in pure strength. Mack had illusion like me, although his was only a variation of it, not the full thing. I didn't have any limits with what I could do, while he could only make copies of things. Of course, all my friends could be hiding more abilities like I was, but that's all I knew about their powers, all they ever showed.

"Welcome to Twelfth Year Guard Class," Professor Garrick called as he walked onto the mats. He had been our instructor every year, so we knew his expectations by now. All of us were standing in a straight line, waiting. The training arena was located farthest from the ocean, which was another reason it was our last class of the day. It took the longest to walk to.

"This is your most important year to date. You will be challenged and tested at every turn. But more importantly, today marks the start of the Six Battles."

Everyone straightened on the mats. We've been preparing for this moment our entire schooling. The Six Battles were a big fucking deal that happened at the start of term and only twelfth years could compete.

To get picked as the final six meant an advantage during your Trials and whoever won was guaranteed a spot in Palm. Each of the six Tennebrisian schools selects six competitors to spar in the competition.

The only schools that didn't take it seriously were LakeWood and Narway—but that was only because they'd never won before.

My brother came in first his year, and I planned to do the same.

The battles were notorious for having the most brutal fights, even more than the Trials themselves. It was also why Lilia was here. Twelfth year was the only year that combined Guard and Mending classes. Because if you made it to the Six Battles, you were guaranteed to get the shit beaten out of you.

"The first competition will take place in three weeks," Professor Garrick continued. "Since that doesn't give us a lot of time, training must start immediately. By the end of class today, we will have our competitors." A murmur went out across us before Garrick silenced it. We knew this was coming. We'd been preparing for it just as much as our Trials. "You have ten minutes to warm up," he said, looking between us. "Then I want you back on the mats to find out who has what it takes to be Kitlarn's Six."

My friends and I smiled at each other because if there was one thing I was certain of, it was that we were all going to be a part of the Six.

SIX
LILIA

PETER WAS right about the attention. I hated it. People were constantly staring at me, and whenever I shared a class with Greyland, I knew they were looking at him too. The talk about Sie Noren and Scotlind Rumor wasn't dying down, especially after they finished their tour.

I wasn't sure what I heard more of—gossip about Grey and I, or the fact that a zero was selected for Sie. Kitlarn was wealthy. It shouldn't have shocked me that most people in our town would hate Scotlind for becoming the queen.

I found myself smiling and liking her more. But whenever I heard the conversation shift to Greyland, it would wipe the smile right off my face. Grace and Jaxs made it into a game—they were counting how many girls talked about going after him now that his older brother was taken. Greyland Noren was the next best thing, and I absolutely hated it.

I convinced myself that it was only because I hated *him*.

And now, watching him fight, it was easy to remember why. It wasn't like Greyland gave me any thought. He barely looked at me during school and made it a point to wholly ignore me. When I was younger, it used to piss me off. Every school year, I used to run to

Peter and cry to him about it. I couldn't understand why him and Sie were friends, but Greyland wouldn't be mine.

Grace and I watched the sparring from the sidelines. Professor Garrick called it a free for all, and it was a shit show. Was this what my brother went through when he fought in the Six Battles with Sie?

Everyone was fighting on the mats at once. It was a mix of abilities and physical fighting. The rules were simple: when you couldn't fight anymore, you were out. The last six students standing were the final six.

I watched as Lander and Colton fought together. I couldn't tell where the real Mack was because he had his clones scattered around the gym, fighting multiple students at once. But it was Greyland I couldn't take my eyes off of. He was by himself. I knew he was using his illusion, but he was moving so fast it was hard to tell what he was doing and who he was using it on. Everyone who came up against the four of them didn't last long.

By the end of the hour, Grace and I mended eight classmates. Three of them were because of Lander. I was still wrapping Hilton's arm when Professor Garrick called everyone back to the center of the mats.

"The final six are Colton Ali, Lander Autions, Trenton Bree, Mack Futon, Chase Michael, and Greyland Noren." There was a slow clap that went around the room. I kept my eyes trained on the gauze I was tying around Hilton, forcing myself not to look up at Greyland as Professor Garrick kept talking. "Our first match will be against Backerly in three weeks. The six of you will train every weekend until the Six Battles are finished."

I was doing an okay job at avoiding Greyland, but when Professor Garrick dismissed the class, I couldn't help it. I looked up. He was drenched in sweat. The white training uniform he was wearing became somewhat translucent.

His dark eyes met mine for a split second before I forced myself to look away.

———

"You like watching me fight, Lil." Dream-Greyland smirked as he sat down next to me on the green sofa. "Admit it."

"I do not." I could feel my cheeks reddening even as I denied it.

"You were watching me though."

I rolled my eyes. "I was watching everyone. I had to in order to assess for any injuries."

His smirked turned into a full blown smile, and I hated how much I loved it.

"Why do you want to be a guard?" I asked. I knew about ninety percent of Advenians Trialing for the guard only did it because they wanted a better chance of getting accepted into a future King's Tournament. But with Sie on the throne, I couldn't fathom Greyland going up against his own brother. I knew the two of them were close.

Dream-Grey shrugged. "I want to leave Kitlarn, and my chances of being stationed in Palm are high as a guard."

I looked at him. "That's the only reason? So you can leave Kitlarn?"

He sighed as he leaned back into the sofa. "Since my father is in Kitlarn, it's a good enough reason for me."

I nodded, not sure how to respond to that. I hated Greyland's father. It honestly wasn't a shock that Greyland in real life turned out to be such a dick. He was raised by one. I knew their household was cruel and lacked love.

"What are you thinking about, Lil?" he asked after a moment.

"Do you want a family of your own someday?"

"Why is that what's on your mind?" He turned to look at me.

"Because if you become a guard it means you can't have a family. Guards are discouraged from getting married, and they aren't allowed to have kids. Is leaving Kitlarn really more important than all of that?"

He was quiet for a minute. "If I were to take a wife, it'd be one my father picked out for me. So no, I don't want a family."

"You can marry anyone you want, Grey. Once you graduate, your father won't be able to dictate your life."

He shook his head. "My mother," he started, then stopped and cleared his throat. "He'll get me to do whatever he wants because of her. If I refuse, she'll be the one to suffer. It's just easier—"

Suddenly, my body was freezing.

"Lilia, wake up." Grace used her telekinesis to pull my blanket off and was hovering it in the middle of our room.

I groaned. How was I the only Advenian who actually liked sleep? I squinted my eyes open and glanced at the clock.

"Goddess, Grace, why are you up? It's five in the morning. The dining hall isn't even open yet. I told you for years now that if there isn't tea, I'm not getting up."

I was having a good dream too...

"Professor Lynn posted our assignments for the Six Battles. Don't you want to know which ones we're going to?"

I perked up. I did want to know. Ever since the Six were declared, I'd been wracking my brain for when I'd have to mend them. The first match was now only two weeks away.

"Ugh, fine," I groaned as I forced myself out of bed. "But you owe me the biggest cup of tea imaginable."

"Deal." Grace grinned.

The schedule for the Six Battles was posted outside the Mender's Building. Luckily, it was only three buildings down from the dining hall, so we would still be meeting Jaxson by the time the hall opened.

There were nine menders that signed up for Guard Classes as their volunteer work, which meant we were all rotating travel for the Six Battles. We'd each have to mend two different matches, and I couldn't tell if I wanted to be assigned for away fights or home ones. If we got sent to the other villages, it meant I would get to see more of Tennebris. I had only ever been in Kitlarn, and the idea of traveling exhilarated me. But that also meant it was more time spent with Greyland and his friends. We would be forced to travel together, and as much as I wanted to see Tennebris, I couldn't tell if it was worth being around the four of them any longer than I had to.

"Yay, we're together!" Grace beamed as she scanned the paper. "It's me, you, and Nash for our assignments."

"Let me see," I said as I stepped in front of her, and then leaned forward on my toes to get a better look. We were going to mend the first match—Kitlarn against Backerly—and it was away. I looked down at the other five matches. Our names were listed again for the home match—Kitlarn against Addler.

It was the best I could hope for. One away and one home. But it meant I'd have to travel with Greyland and his friends—and soon.

SEVEN
GREYLAND

We were all shoved into a van that was taking us to the monorail at the ass crack of dawn. Our first match was against Backerly and it was on their turf. I'd been to five of the six villages in Tennebris before simply because I wanted to—it was one of the luxuries of having a vehicle and an endless supply of electricity to run it. I often left home for the weekend, just to get away, but I never drove through Backerly. I didn't want to risk getting stuck on their mountain pass, so I was keen to see the full breadth of their village.

Grace, Lilia, and a guy named Nash were the menders selected to come with us today. I hated that Lilia was coming to the match furthest away. Backerly took over half a day's travel, and even with the speed of the monorail, we wouldn't get back to Kitlarn until after nightfall.

My father sent a letter to the school, which I immediately threw in the fire after I read it. *"Win your match. If you get injured, stay home."*

I scoffed. Of course that was all he cared about. My brother's wedding to Scotlind Rumor was in one week, and if I took a beating during the battles, he wouldn't let me attend. Goddess forbid, I showed up with a black eye and the Noren name looked weak.

Lilia dozed off during the ride over to the rail and the prick, Nash, was smiling as she accidentally leaned against his shoulder. Grace seemed oblivious to the fact that she was letting her best friend fall asleep on some random dude… but maybe he wasn't random. They were taking mending classes together, and I knew nothing about her personal life.

"We're here," I announced loudly. I didn't wait to see if Lilia woke up or how she reacted to finding out she had been sleeping on the guy. I left the van before I could see any of it and started storming toward the rail, waiting for the doors to open.

I used to ride in it with my brother when we were younger, but that was before he got his car. And now that I had my own, I never used public transportation. I loved driving, and I loved the solitude. I wanted nothing more than to be able to drive myself to these battles, to feel the wind against my face and have nothing but open road in front of me.

"It's freezing as balls here," Mack said as he came up behind me. We were at the edge of the shield, making the area frozen and snow-laden. The rail entrance to Kitlarn was between the woods and the ocean. The location was just shy of the school, making the need for vans necessary.

"Yeah. It's all snow for miles," I murmured as I scanned the beach in front of us. I knew if you followed the coast three miles down, it led to a private cove with black sand hidden beneath mounds of snow.

"How do you know?" Mack asked, rubbing his hands together for warmth.

I shrugged. "I used to explore Kitlarn by foot before I was old enough to drive." While my brother and Peter liked to explore the woods to escape our home, I came here.

I followed my friends onto the rail and tried not to think about what Grace, Lilia, and Nash were doing in their own compartment.

Having no intention of listening to Lander talk about how he planned on beating the living shit out of Backerly's Six, I tried to drift off to sleep. Goddess knows I needed it.

———

I WOKE up by the time we made it into Backerly. I only knew we were close because the landscape shifted and the monorail started traveling up a steep incline. The town itself was built into the crests of mountains.

Professor Garrick barged into our compartment. "Get ready. We need to be back at the school tonight, so you boys are fighting immediately."

A vehicle was waiting outside the monorail in Backerly to take us the rest of the way to the school. We all crammed inside it, and I was forced to watch as Nash took a seat next to Lilia. He kept leaning toward her, and whatever he whispered made her giggle.

"What's wrong, Grey?" Mack asked. He was sitting next to me.

I rolled my shoulders, forcing my gaze away from her. "Nothing. Just can't concentrate."

"You better focus." Lander smirked. "Wouldn't want you to miss the royal wedding."

I gritted my teeth. Sharing a suite with Lander was the worst thing to come out of this year so far. Not only because I hated him, but he was a nosey prick and read my note over my shoulder before I realized it.

"What are you talking about?" Colton asked.

"Nothing—" I said, at the same time Lander answered, "Daddy Noren sent Grey a note saying if he lost his match he wouldn't be allowed to go to the wedding."

"Really?" Colton's eyes widened. "Sie's your brother. That's fucked if you don't get to go."

It took me a moment before I realized Lilia had stopped talking to Nash and was staring at me. Right. I was her ticket to the wedding. If I didn't go, she couldn't.

"Good thing I don't plan on losing then."

"WELCOME to the first of the Six Battles," Backerly's guard professor —Opal—announced. We were standing outside, on top of a peak that had its top carved out to resemble flat terrain. "You will all be fighting to represent your school. Each match will be tallied, and a mark will be given to the school of the winning contestant. Your marks will carry over all your matches. The school with the most marks at the end of the Battles will be the winner."

Professor Garrick stepped forward. "All six fighters from the winning school will have their victory added to their school records for the Trials. Even though your wins ultimately count toward your school, you will also be judged individually. By the end of the Battles, the professors will select one elite fighter to be the Champion Six. That individual will have a one way ticket to being a guard in Palm. The Champion Six doesn't have to come from the winning school. So don't forget, you are fighting for your school, but you're also fighting for yourselves."

"We will select your opponent at random," Professor Opal called over the wind. Backerly was at the highest elevation where the shield was the weakest, and I already didn't mind never visiting this place on my own. "Abilities and physical fighting are both encouraged. I expect you all studied your handbooks by now and have memorized it for the matches. No serious injuries as depicted in the handbook are permitted or you'll be disqualified and your school will fight the rest of their battles short one contestant."

"I want Acker," Lander whispered as Professor Opal started reciting the rules.

"Why?" Mack asked.

"Because he has energy weaponry like Lander," I answered for him.

"And that makes you want to fight him?" Colton frowned as he looked up at the six opponents we'd be fighting today.

"I want to prove I'm better, so yeah."

"First match—Chase Michael, fighting from Kitlarn, against Matthew Billard, fighting from Backerly," Opal hollered.

I watched two matches before my name was called. Lander was pissed when Acker was selected as my opponent. I honestly wanted Lander to fight him—not because I couldn't handle him—but because

Acker was known as Backerly's top contestant, and I wanted nothing more than to see Lander get his ass handed to him.

I also *hated* fighting against energy weaponry. Fucking hated the ability.

"Don't get a nick on your pretty little face, Grey," Lander teased as I walked toward the ring.

Yeah, this didn't bode well for the whole not-getting-beaten-up part, but I was going to my brother's wedding. There was no way I was losing.

I immediately called to my ability. The key was to slowly and subtly shift into an illusion. Anyone that sucked using illusion always did it too quickly.

I was at a disadvantage being at an away match—the guy I was up against knew his training grounds better than I did—but I'd been subtly memorizing them from the moment I arrived.

I started with small changes. Sounds were always easier for me. I blocked out one classmate cheering us on, then two, then added in a fake noise from another. Chaotic diversion. It took awhile to master altering my surroundings while maintaining complete focus of my own. In order to win, I had to physically fight my opponents while I crafted the illusion, and Acker materialized a freaking axe. If I wasn't as fast as I was, I would have lost an arm. Which there was no way Lilia or any of the other menders would have been able to fix.

I started shifting my illusion onto myself. It was the hardest to pull off when Acker never took his eyes off me.

I started with an inch here and there, pretending to take a step in my illusion, when in reality, I hadn't moved. Acker's vision was slowly shifting, a step left, then right, a fake counter. The more we fought, the more I altered.

I hadn't read the handbook for the fights, but I didn't need to. I knew the gist of what to expect from watching my brother and Peter compete in their year. It was similar to the Trials—a knockout, a surrender, or scoring more points within the allotted time. The only difference between the two was that our Trials had two minutes of fighting, where the battles gave us six. Everything was six to the point where I started to hate the number.

Six competitors, six schools, six matches for a total of six minutes each.

I swore as Acker sliced my stomach with the dagger he was now holding before I let my illusion completely unfold. I was done winning by physical blows. I let Acker fight air, pretending I was still dodging him as I moved toward the edge of the ring and waited.

I could have attacked him from behind and ended the match right away, but there was a twisted sort of joy in letting him *think* he won. My illusion was only on Acker. Everyone else saw me standing to the side of the ring with my hands in my pocket while my opponent went crazy fighting against nothing.

I always wanted to be able to freeze time so I could constantly relive the feeling when I let my illusion fade. Acker's face shifted from the version of me he thought was in front of him, to the real me standing off to the side. It was intoxicating, watching his face drain of color as anger took over his features, and he realized he'd been fighting nothing but air.

I smirked as I left the ring, knowing I already won before Professor Opal announced it.

"Grey, go see a mender," Professor Garrick called.

I looked down and saw my white uniform was stained red across my abdomen. Fuck. I forgot that Acker nicked me before I fully set my illusion. "I'm fine."

"I don't care if you tell me you're made of glitter. I gave you an order, now go."

I ground my teeth together when I saw Lilia was the only free mender. Grace was finishing up with Chase, and Nash was doing Goddess knows what.

"What do you need?" Lilia asked when she spotted me.

"Aren't you supposed to tell me?" I mused.

Her brows furrowed. I knew she was watching my fight, and even if she wasn't, my bright red abdomen was enough of a tell-tale sign of what was injured.

"Sit," she ordered, instead of taking the bait.

I sank onto the stool she pointed to and started unbuttoning my shirt, watching as Lilia pivoted to prepare gauze and whatever else she thought I'd need.

Her hazel eyes flared when she turned back around. She dropped what she was holding. "What... What are you doing?"

"I figured you needed to actually see the wound you're about to mend." I arched my brow, amused as her face became redder than my stomach. Maybe getting sliced wasn't so bad after all.

And the fact that it was hidden beneath my clothes meant I could still go to Sie's wedding next weekend. I won my fight, and Acker didn't land a hit that would show. I'd call that a win.

"Right." She bent down and started picking up whatever she dropped when Nash came up behind her.

"Here, let me get that," he said as he bent over her, resting his hand across her back. "I'll mend him." He still hadn't moved his hand. "You can get the next one."

"Oh-okay." Lilia bolted away from me faster than I could blink, and I tried not to be offended. The idea of Lilia assisting anyone else had me seeing red, and the fact that Lander was up next for sparring was pissing me off. I wanted to punch Nash in his Goddess damn throat as I watched Lilia stare blindly at the ring.

I hissed as he pressed the gauze into my stomach with more force than he should have. I turned my focus away from Lilia and Lander to see his eyes narrowed.

"What's your deal with Lilia?" I asked. I couldn't get the image of her sleeping on his shoulder out of my head.

"Why do you care?"

"I don't," I said coolly. "My brother—"

"Yeah, save me the bullshit," he cut me off.

"Excuse me?"

Nash was tying the end of my gauze together, the fabric already started to soak through with my blood. "Everyone knows that your brother is friends with Lilia's brother. I'm not stupid."

"What's that supposed to mean?"

"It means half the Advenians in our year won't make a move on Lilia because of your idle threats. Anyone who tries backs off the instant you give them a pissing contest and scare the shit out of them."

I was silent for a moment. I hadn't even realized I did that, but now that he said it, I couldn't deny it. I had been grilling Nash down the moment I saw him with Lilia.

"So yeah," Nash continued as he stood and wiped my blood off his hands, "I'm not scared of you, and whatever threat you're about to make won't stop me from talking to her."

"Fuck off," I spat as I rose from the stool.

"I'll fuck whoever I want, Greyland," he said before walking off.

I tried not to seethe or show that Nash's words pissed me off to no end. Lilia could date whoever she wanted.

I didn't care.

Kitlarn won—four to two. Mack and Trenton were the only ones who lost their matches, and I sent a silent thanks to Pylemo that Lilia didn't have to mend Lander.

EIGHT
LILIA

"ARE YOU NERVOUS FOR TOMORROW?"

"Why would I be nervous?" I snapped.

My dream version of Greyland shrugged as he slumped onto our usual sofa. "We're going to Palm where the most narcissistic Advenians live—"

"And because I don't have any abilities, I should be scared?" I finished for him.

"Maybe." His response surprised me. It wasn't malicious or meant to harass me, but he looked more concerned than anything else. Well, duh. It was my own subconscious that was worried—he wasn't real. "You're going to be in a room full of the strongest Advenians, not only from Palm but from all of Tennebris. Not to mention the entire High Council will be there."

Tomorrow Greyland and I were excused from classes to attend the Royal Wedding. Since his brother was the future king and mine was his future second, we were given permission to go. I was honestly excited. I missed my brother, and I couldn't wait to see him again. It hadn't crossed my mind that I should be worried about it until now.

"Your brother is marrying a rank zero. She's living in the castle, are you going to warn her too?" I diverted, instead of answering.

Greyland laughed, and I couldn't decipher what he found so funny.

"What?" I asked, when he still didn't answer.

"I don't need to warn her about anything."

"So I'm the only rank zero that needs to worry about being in Palm?" I snapped. Peter told me that Scotlind trained to be a guard before she was selected for Sie, but just because I didn't know how to fight, didn't mean I was helpless.

"I'm not saying she doesn't need to worry. I'm sure she does. The reason I don't need to warn her is because she has my brother to look out for her."

"Oh," I said, my cheeks reddening, then I thought more on it. "Right, and I don't have anyone to look out for me."

"Your brother will be there," he replied.

I must have frowned because he asked, "What's wrong?"

I met his dark stare. This was *my* dream for crying out loud. I was supposed to be able to control it. I didn't want reality to seep into my sleep. I wanted a freaking escape.

"What if I don't want my brother watching me?"

"Nash won't be there," he snapped, his tone shifting.

I was taken aback for a moment, having no idea how to respond. "Nash?"

"The mender you were cozying up to during the first Six Battles."

I started laughing. "Goddess, no. I don't want Nash."

Shock coursed through him, so subtly, I only knew because I stared at him every night—studied him so thoroughly that I felt like I truly knew him. Of course, it wasn't the real him. Greyland in real life was an asshole. But this Greyland, this version of him—

He swallowed, and I watched his throat bob. "Who do you want?"

I knew what he would expect me to say. Peter always teased me growing up, claiming I liked Sie, but I didn't. I just never corrected him because it was better than Grey knowing the truth. I've had a crush on Greyland Aaron Noren for as long as I could remember. I didn't want to. I hated him, hated that I liked him, hated that I still liked him after everything he's done to me. But I couldn't stop it, just like I couldn't stop dreaming about him every night.

"What if..." I started and stopped. He couldn't reject me in my own dream. I found his gaze again, found that he wasn't moving, wasn't even breathing. "What if I want *you*?"

It was quiet for so long. In my dream, the silence was worse than reality. There was nothing. No distractions, not even the distant dripping of rain or the soft hum of wind. It was still. And as I waited, I wondered if maybe I didn't have a grip on my own dreams. Maybe Greyland would reject me even in my mind.

But then he leaned forward. His coarse hand found my cheek, and I shivered at how cold it felt, how real it all was. I even mapped out the feeling of his calluses—how they would feel as they grazed against me before wrapping around the back of my neck.

His breath was minty as he exhaled, like he had been holding it and everything let out at once. I closed my eyes, waiting to feel his lips against mine—

"Lilia, you're going to be late." Grace had used her telekinesis to rip my blankets off my body again. Well that explained the shivers in my dream and why I felt so cold... "Honestly, I think you'd sleep the day away if I never woke you."

I groaned. Grace was my own personal walking, and very annoying, alarm clock. "I was having a good dream."

"Well, Greyland is going to be picking you up in an hour, and you need to get dressed for the wedding."

I sat up straight, my back going rigid. Everything came rushing back to me. My cheeks heated as I recalled every detail of my dream. But then it immediately sank once I realized I would be seeing said person really soon, and he would be nothing like I dreamt.

"Go bathe, and I'll pick out a dress for you to wear," Grace said before using her powers to throw my blanket back onto my bed. She wasn't one for fashion. Grace didn't care about how she looked, but her parents did, and the girl had an immense wardrobe because of it. And lucky for me, because if it wasn't for her, I would be wearing my school uniform to the Royal Wedding.

I was excited to see my brother. I was excited to finally meet Scotlind Rumor too. I'd never been to a wedding before, and I had no idea what to expect. I kept recalling Dream-Greyland's warning—*I should be worried.*

"I wish you were coming with me," I told Grace.

She rolled her eyes. They were a pale brown, striking against her olive skin and golden hair.

"To spend an entire evening forced to dress up for the very people who put our society into the shambles that it is today and pretend that everything is fine with their egotistical logic? No, thank you. I'll take my evening with Jaxs and live vicariously through you when you come back."

I huffed a laugh as I gathered my stuff for the communal bath. Yeah, I had the best friend in the entire world.

———

MY HEART WAS in my throat by the time I was ready for Greyland to pick me up. The dress Grace let me borrow fit me surprisingly well. It was only slightly tight but worked in my favor by hugging my hips. It was a dark green that brought out the smear of coloring I had in my eyes. I threw my navy school coat on top, covering the dress because, although it was beautiful, the silk did little to keep me warm.

Grace and I both attempted to do my makeup and after spending the remaining time trying to do something—anything—to my hair, we decided to leave it down. I was speechless when she surprised me with a new pair of heels. They were black with a wedge thick enough that I found them easy to walk in.

"Grace, what is this?" I had asked earlier, my eyes widening.

"Consider it an early birthday present." My friend grinned.

"My birthday isn't for another two months."

"I know. That's why I said *early.*"

"I can't accept these." I knew to her family a new pair of shoes was nothing, but to me, it was everything. I'd gone through years where I was forced to wear Peter's hand-me-downs that were two sizes too big with part of the sole missing.

"You can, and you will. Besides, I have no use for them. They won't fit me, and there is no way you are ruining that dress with your school shoes."

I had planned on wearing my uniform shoes, which would have shown considering the dress stopped just before my calves.

"Grace, I—"

"Just say thank you and tell me all about it when you come back."

And now, I was standing by the parking deck, my new shoes barely visible through the long coat, while I waited for Grey.

This was going to be the longest I'd be alone with Greyland—besides in my dreams. He was taking me to Palm, which was a little under half a day's ride away.

Before last week, I'd never left Kitlarn. Before this week, I wasn't sure if I was going to ever again. The only way I would was if I got assigned to another village after my Trials. And it didn't really matter what my results were—servants, cooks, and menders were needed in all six towns—the chances of them moving me away from Kitlarn were slim to none.

I knew my invitation to the wedding was Peter's doing. He alone was the reason I was allowed to attend tonight. I was proud of him. It was still so surreal that he was going to be the second in Tennebris. My parents always knew it was a possibility. Everyone from Kitlarn was confident Sie would one day become king. We just weren't sure if his father's influence would affect who he chose as his second. Unlike Greyland, Sie didn't have any friends. Peter was his only one, and regardless of how strong my brother was, our family lineage wasn't.

My parents weren't attending. Not because they weren't invited, because they were. They just claimed they had too much to do, but I saw through it. My parents were never busy. Besides their work, they had dinner together every night and always went on the same walk around Kitlarn afterward. It was their nightly ritual.

But I knew the real reason they weren't coming was the cost. They spent everything they had to send me to school, and the travel fees alone to get to Palm would be a year's worth of savings.

The only reason I was going was because, by some miracle, Greyland agreed to drive me. Well, I was certain that miracle had to do with our mothers, and he didn't actually have a choice, but regardless, I was happy. Even if it meant I had to spend hours alone with him in his car.

I heard the roar of the engine before I saw him. My heart stopped as his car jutted to a halt in front of me, blowing up the ends of my coat.

Nerves started wracking my body, and I couldn't convince myself that it was because of Dream-Grey's warning. My hands were trembling, and my breathing was in shambles by the time I opened the passenger door and threw my bag in between my legs. Last night's dream came crashing back to me. I almost kissed him. I mean, my dream-self did, but I felt like Greyland could see through me, like it was written all over my face that I dreamt about him.

It was the first time it happened. We only ever talked before in my dreams, and I still couldn't believe I almost kissed him. It never went that far before and now it was all I could think about. I kept staring at his hands gripping the wheel, wondering if I imagined his callouses right and how they would really feel embedded through my hair. I hated that I wanted him in my dreams.

But what I hated even more was that, for the first time, I wanted him to kiss me now, *in real life*.

"Ready?" he asked after a moment. His voice was taut, and his hand tightened around the steering wheel.

I nodded, unable to find my words.

By the time we made it to the castle, I had to pee, but I wasn't about to ask him to stop, so I crossed my legs and sucked it up, cursing myself for drinking too much tea beforehand.

The road was mostly through the woods. I couldn't see much beyond frost covered trees out of the window. We didn't even pass another vehicle until we entered Palm.

I knew before Greyland told me that we were here. The town was built differently than Kitlarn. Everything was packed together, more vertical, while our town was spread out. It gave the feeling of claustrophobia and grime even though everything was pristine. There were still trees, but the forest at our backs started thinning.

My mouth gaped open as we turned a corner, and the castle came into view. It was massive. The summer sun was bright as I squinted against the sandstone pillars. Greyland drove the car to the back where a large lake was looming in the distance.

I'd been staring at his hands throughout the drive, and although his voice came out relaxed, his grip was still menacing against the leather wheel, his knuckles a shade paler from where he gripped it. "We're here, *Little*."

Little. The nickname he used for me in real life, not Lil like he often said in my dreams.

"You know I can call you *Little* too," I said as I got out of the car.

He eyed me. "I don't call you little because you're Peter's sister." Everyone else did. I was Little Fervic and he was Little Noren—the younger siblings to Sie and Peter. "And nothing about me is little," he added.

I almost tripped over the pebbled path when my mind went in the wrong direction, and my traitorous eyes drifted over his pants.

He smirked as he noticed, and I forced my gaze away, taking in the rest of him. He was in a deep-set suit, the color was darker than navy but lighter than black. It fit him perfectly, like it was tailored to his exact body—I rolled my eyes—it probably was tailored to fit him.

"I'm not *little* either."

He stepped toward me then, and I got a front row view of exactly what he meant. Greyland was tall, all the Norens were. I swore he'd grown another inch since last summer. I had to crane my neck to look at him even in my heels, and I was average height for an Advenian girl.

"You are to me," he said, his voice silky. "Let's go. I'm supposed to take you to Peter before the ceremony starts." He started walking toward the castle, leaving me gaping after him.

NINE
GREYLAND

Lilia and I walked through the halls in silence. I'd been to the castle a few times before, just not as much as Peter and Sie growing up. My dad used to drag me along before I realized I wanted nothing to do with it. A simple request from my mom, and I was allowed to stay home. They were my favorite memories growing up, when she really came out of her shell, and I got a small glimpse of what a loving household could look like. It was a guilt I always carried whenever I saw Sie. He never got that. He never got to see that side of her.

Now, as we walked through the halls, it felt ominous. Lilia took everything in at my side. I had no idea what she was thinking. I didn't think it was awe that had her hazel eyes drifting from looming fireplaces to the scarce chandeliers dropping from the ceiling. Everything was cold and somber here. Despite the attempt to make it cheerful, the stained-glass windows added color into the space, but it still couldn't fix what the castle was—dark.

When we finally made it to the second floor landing by Peter's room, I planned on leaving her to go to my own. We only had thirty minutes before the ceremony, plenty of time to drop off my bags and get a drink. If I knew my brother, he probably left a bottle of our favorite red wine in the suite I was staying in.

I had no idea if Lilia was staying in Peter's room because she wanted to or if she had to. Sie secured my room at the castle tonight, and I didn't even ask how much it would cost—didn't even cross my mind. But I knew it did to the Fervics.

I watched for five long seconds as Lilia jumped into her brother's arms before I turned to bolt out of the room.

"Little Noren," Peter called behind me, "wait up. I need tc talk to you."

I turned in time to see him set Lilia's feet back onto the ground. Her hair was in her face, blocking her eyes as she blew the loose strands away, while Peter was grinning from ear to ear. Sometimes I hated how happy the two of them were. I loved my brother, but the relationship between Peter and Lilia always made me envious. It was carefree and fun. They didn't have to protect each other. Peter didn't have to take beatings for Lilia. Their parents loved them even if they couldn't afford to.

Lilia's grin faltered as her gaze met mine. Her smile wasn't as wide as her brother's and it definitely wasn't used nearly as much—at least not around me. Peter's deep dimples were sunken permanently into his cheeks, but Lilia's... hers were seldom. It made my breath catch whenever I saw them. They were softer and shallow, making sure you worked for the joy they provoked.

"What's up?" I looked at Peter. I was finally taller than him, not that height ever mattered to him. He could shapeshift into anything, and I'd never met anything or anyone that intimidated him. Not even my brother or my dad, which half of Tennebris was afraid of.

He glanced down at Lilia. "In private."

"Alright," I said as I followed him out into the hall. I caught a glimpse of Lilia putting her small, tattered bag onto her brother's bed before the door shut behind me.

"I need you to watch Lilia tonight."

"No," I said immediately.

"I'm not asking, Greyland." Peter's expression was serious, and he almost never called me by my real name. "I'm begging you to. I'm going to be stuck with Sie and Scotlind all night. I won't be able to watch her myself. You remember when you used to come here with us when we were younger?"

I nodded, not sure how I could forget.

"And do you remember Alec?"

I nodded again. The guy was a total tool. I'd overheard Peter and Sie complain about him, but I didn't need their opinions to make my own. He was one of the worst Advenians I'd ever met. He honestly reminded me of Lander, just older so he had more time to develop his cruelness.

"He's going to be at the wedding," Peter continued. "Word got out that my sister was coming tonight, and he knows she's projected to be a zero. I—" he stopped. Took a breath. "Lilia's never been compelled before..."

"So you're asking me to babysit her so Alec doesn't compel her?" I huffed, feigning indifference, but his words kept hitting me. I never thought about it before, that she's never been compelled. It would immediately tell her if she was actually a zero. I knew she was secretly holding onto hope that she wasn't, that she prayed she had some minor ability that wasn't obvious, and the idea of that reality being crushed for her in front of an entire crowd of ruthless Advenians struck a nerve with me.

"Yes." He looked me right in the eye. "Please."

"No," I said after a minute. I hated myself for it, hated how stubborn I was. But I never protected her at school, so I wasn't about to start now. Besides, it wasn't like Alec was going to compel Lilia in front of everyone.

"Grey, there's something else. It's not just Alec I'm worried about." Peter shifted, his voice dropping to a whisper. "There was an attack on Scotlind."

"Shit," I cursed. "When?"

"About a month ago. Thank the Goddess there hasn't been another one yet, but the guard who attacked her escaped."

"And you're worried it wasn't a lone incident, that there might be another attack tonight?"

He turned to look down the hall, and I knew he was checking to make sure we were still alone. "I don't know. I doubt they will attack Scottie in front of so many people. Plus your brother isn't planning on leaving her alone tonight, but..."

"You think it might have been because she has no powers."

He nodded. "I have no idea if it's because she's marrying your brother or if it's because she's a zero, but I don't want to leave Lilia unprotected in case it's the latter."

"Why did you agree to bring her then?" I asked, pissed off that Lilia was even here. If our mothers arranged for me to drive her, it would have taken one simple conversation from Peter to stop it.

"Because I want a better future for her. If I didn't let her come, it would have been obvious that it was because I thought she was weak. The entire High Council will be attending tonight and if I want a chance at her not being a servant—" he paused, and I could see the dilemma written across his face. "She's always going to be vulnerable, Greyland, but I don't want Lilia to ever think that."

"Why me?" I asked, already knowing my answer. I could under-stand his reasoning for bringing her, not that I agreed with it. She was going to end up a servant no matter how hard either of them tried to deny it.

"There isn't anyone else I trust," he admitted.

"You know Lilia won't like it. She's not going to agree to stay with me, and I don't feel like chasing her all night."

"Leave that to me."

"Fine," I snapped as I walked back into Peter's room. Lilia's eyes widened, not expecting me. Her coat was off now, and I nearly choked on my own spit. She was in a sleeveless dress that hid little of her body, which I found myself enjoying for a total of ten seconds before I realized everyone else was going to see it too.

I had no idea where she got the money for the dress, but fuck me, it was the most divine thing I ever saw. It hit her curves in a way that showed just enough while still making me crave more.

I readjusted myself in my pants, pissed off and embarrassed that someone—especially her—was getting to me this easily. Thank

Pylemo Peter didn't notice because I would have been dead on the floor if he did.

It made me realize what Peter asked me to do was necessary. The girl was delusional. She was stuck in her own personal bubble, completely unaware that anyone could and would use her if they wanted. It had me second guessing if I agreed to watch her because of the threat to zeroes or if I just didn't want anyone else looking at her tonight.

"What is he still doing here—" she started.

"You're staying with Greyland tonight."

"What?" She whirled on her brother. "Why can't I sleep here?"

Peter's eyes flared. "Ew, Lilia, relax, that's not what I meant. You're staying in my room." He let out a laugh. "I'd kill Grey very slowly if you two ever shared a bed."

"Oh." Her cheeks flushed as she avoided my gaze.

"I meant at the ceremony."

"I'm not a child anymore, Peter—"

"Your wrist isn't burned yet, Lil. That quite literally means you're still a child."

Her eyes narrowed, and I couldn't hide the smirk on my lips. "Neither is Grey's, so I don't see how he's any better."

"For one, he's a guy, and I know this sucks to hear, but people aren't going to try to fuck him, and two, he isn't wearing a revealing dress." Her lips smacked together, and I knew she was about to interrupt, but Peter kept going, "He's also a Noren and no one will try to mess with that name. We don't have the luxury."

I couldn't help but notice how he never mentioned it was because she was a zero.

"If you want to be at the celebration, that's my rule. Just because you're here, doesn't mean you have to attend. I could assign some guards to watch the door while you stay in my room all night."

She crossed her arms over her chest, and I had to look away to not stare at what she was drawing attention to. I was acting like I'd never seen boobs before. It wasn't like Lilia's were anything special...

"Fine," she ground out. "I'll stay with Grey."

I needed that glass of red wine an hour ago...

———

SCOTLIND RUMOR—WELL, I guess Scotlind *Noren* now—looked beautiful. I knew my brother thought the same thing. He couldn't tear his gaze away from her. We were still in the throne room, only now it was transformed from a wedding ceremony to a reception.

My brother and his wife were sitting together on a dais. Their hands were still bound with a small puddle of blood on the floor between them. I still couldn't believe they forced the blood bond on them. I knew Sie wasn't expecting it. The Tennebrisians who won the King's Tournament in the past were already married—my brother was the youngest to ever take the crown, so he was probably one of the few who hadn't already taken a bride, but I was still shocked as hell when they did it.

There was a long line of guests waiting to greet my brother, and other than a smile from across the room, I hadn't been able to talk to him. I figured I wouldn't get to.

Lilia was two glasses into champagne, while I was four into wine. I had no idea if she ever drank before. We never hung out at school, and I found myself curious how she spent her time with Grace and Jaxson. Did she drink with them? Did she go to parties in Jelckin?

I kept shifting my gaze through the room and anytime a male glanced her way, I made sure they didn't again. I didn't realize I was using my ability until halfway through the night. Whenever their gazes drifted to the deep cut in her dress, I cast my illusion to give her a turtleneck.

I was really glad I didn't have my brother's powers right now, because if I knew what the lowlifes were thinking as they looked at her, they probably wouldn't be alive.

I silently followed Lilia as she made her way to one of the food tables, trying my damn best to avoid staring at her ass. Honestly, Peter shouldn't have asked me to watch her. I wasn't sure if it was because I'd only ever seen her in our school uniform—which the white button up and ashen pants revealed nothing—or if I just desperately needed to get laid. But I couldn't stop staring at her, couldn't stop thinking about her. Throughout the night, my gaze kept lingering on her lips as she slowly nursed her champagne, and now I was staring like a total creep as she ate a piece of cheese from the assortment tables.

"Little Noren," a low voice drawled that had my back tensing. It wasn't Peter saying it this time. I turned to find myself face to face with Alec. His gaze was fixed on Lilia, and I didn't have time to use my illusion before he was soaking her in. "And this must be Little Fervic." He smiled, and I flexed my fingers as I saw Lilia do the same. "I was told Peter's younger sister was attending tonight, but no one told me you'd be so beautiful."

Alec extended his hand to her. I watched in a mixture of horror and fascination as she pushed the cheese she'd been eating into her hand holding her champagne glass, before wiping it against the silk of her dress, completely staining the fabric. The moment she shook Alec's hand, he pulled her toward him.

"May I have this dance?"

"No," I cut in.

Alec cocked a grin as he acknowledged me. "I wasn't asking you."

"Well, I'm answering."

He fully turned toward me now, finally dropping her hand. "When did you grow balls? Last time I saw you, you were yay-high," he gestured toward my chest, "and following us around like a puppy."

"I grew up."

He looked me up and down. I held his stare, not backing down.

Lilia stepped in front of me, casting a glare before turning toward Alec and smiling sweetly. "I would love to dance."

I grabbed her hand, her freaking cheese squishing between our grip, but I didn't let go. I started dragging her away, not caring how much attention we were drawing.

"Let go of me," she spat. But I kept walking, kept dragging her out of the room. I cast my illusion on her, making it look like Alec had turned toward another girl, when in reality he was staring after us, watching as I dragged her out of the throne room.

"What are you doing?" She tugged against my grip. "I want to go back."

"Too bad. I'm taking you to your room."

"Just because someone asked me to dance?" She was seething now.

I didn't answer. Instead, I kept dragging her through the quiet halls, the music slowly fading behind us.

"My brother didn't say I wasn't allowed to dance with anyone."

"Well, I'm saying it for him. You aren't allowed to dance with anyone. And besides, Alec didn't just want a dance."

"So?"

I stopped walking and whirled on her. We were the only ones in the hall. "You want me to take you back to him?" I spat. "He has compulsion, Lilia. He forces rank zeroes to sleep with him. Is that how you want to lose your virginity?"

She huffed, trying to mask the blush forming over her cheeks. "Who says I'm a vir—"

"Literally everyone. You're the biggest prude at school." I could feel my voice rising with my temper.

"That's not true."

"There's bets on whether or not you and Jaxson slept together," I clipped. I didn't add that almost the entire school bet against it. By year ten, when she still hadn't dated anyone, everyone started talking about it.

"He's just my friend—"

I cut her off again, "There's no such thing as guys being friends with girls, Lilia. Wake up. The guy's in love with you."

Her eyes narrowed. "So if Jaxon were here tonight, would you let *him* dance with me?"

My jaw ticked because I couldn't get myself to respond. The simple answer: no.

"Why do you even care?" she seethed. I hated how much I loved the way she looked when she was mad. The way her nose scrunched at the sides, and her lip pouted.

"I don't."

I meant to grab her wrist again, but she pushed me, my back slamming against the wall. I was shocked for a moment that all I could do was stare at her.

Her eyes were bright, fuming with hatred. "You're the biggest jerk I've ever met."

"I know."

She shoved me again. "You ruined my night."

"I know." My head tilted down to look at her. I didn't realize how close she'd gotten to me until her chest was brushing against mine with each sharp inhale.

I wanted to push her away, but at the same time, I wanted to pull her the rest of the way toward me.

"I hate you."

I grabbed her wrists before she could shove me again, pulling them behind her back. "I know," I said, my voice lowering without meaning to.

She didn't try to pull away. We just stayed there, staring at each other and breathing way too heavily to be considered normal.

She leaned into me, her chest fully pressed against mine now. My hands were still hovering over hers behind her back, but my grip loosened.

She could pull away.

Her lashes fluttered as she did a slow blink, and Goddess damn me, they were the most beautiful eyes I'd ever seen.

Hazel.

My new favorite color, which wasn't exactly a color at all, but a mixture of gold, brown, and green.

They were the color of the tea she drank every morning. Peaceful and undisturbed.

They were sunshine lighting a forest. Beautiful and tranquil.

They were moss overgrown on bark. Captivating and consuming.

They were everything.

I wanted to get lost in them, wanted to see nothing else but her and that Goddess damning gaze—

I was about to move my hands from her back to pull her toward me when the click of heels sounded. Someone was walking down the hall.

Lilia jumped as far away as she could get from me, but it was too late. A blush covered her cheeks, and her breathing was rising and falling rapidly.

I forced my gaze away from her chest and saw Reagan coming down the hall—another one of my brother's friends. She had a scowl on her face before she stopped and took us in. Her gaze flicked from Lilia to me, and I knew she remembered me, and judging from her smirk, I was certain Alec told her exactly who Lilia was.

I silently cursed as I grabbed Lilia's wrist again, only this time, she didn't pull away as I guided her down the hall, far away from any of Sie's friends.

TEN
LILIA

I was still wearing Grace's dress in my dream. Maybe I wasn't ready to give up on the night. Maybe I hoped for a different ending.

I was silent as Dream-Greyland came into view. He had on his suit, but his jacket was off, and his white shirt had two buttons undone, exposing a glimpse of his pale skin beneath. He slumped onto the sofa, waiting. I stood for a few more seconds before I sat down next to him.

I wasn't sure how long we were silent before I said, "You know I hate you in real life."

"I know," his answer came immediately.

More time went on. Greyland watched me intently as I unclasped my heels before bringing my feet onto the sofa. I curled them under me as my dress rode up my thigh, but I didn't bother pushing it back down. After tonight, I didn't have the energy to care. It didn't matter anyway.

His dark eyes were soaking me in. They flicked to my bare thigh for a spilt second, lingering on the two moles I had there before he found my gaze again. No one ever saw them. I was fairly confident no one even knew I had moles, and the realization hit me that I'd never shown anyone my thigh before. Greyland—the real Greyland—told me I was a prude, and the entire school had bets on my sex life.

I huffed.

Maybe he was right.

"What are you thinking about?" he asked me. His voice was gentle, so unlike the real him earlier in the hall.

"It doesn't matter."

"It always matters, Lil."

"I guess I just wish things were different."

He was silent again. His head now staring up at the ceiling—well there wasn't a ceiling exactly. It was an endless void of gray. It kept going up and up, fading into a lighter color as it went. A reminder that this wasn't real.

"I do too," he admitted.

"You do what?" I was too busy staring at him that I'd forgotten what we were talking about.

"I wish things were different."

"Like what?" I knew the real Greyland wouldn't have said that. His life was perfect.

He deflected my question. "You know, for a second there, I thought you were going to kiss me tonight." His voice came out laughing, teasing, but I couldn't find the humor in it.

I whipped my head toward his, my hair falling over my shoulders and onto my lap.

"What?" He smiled. "Did I misread you?"

"I—" I started and stopped. I pulled my legs toward my chest, wrapping my hands around them. "No," I said it so quietly, I barely heard myself.

I was staring at my kneecaps, at how my dress was pooling around the base of my hips. I couldn't meet his gaze, but I felt it. I knew he was watching me. The cushions shifted and a second later his fingers grazed my chin, gently pulling my head up to look at him.

"Lilia." His voice sounded musical. "Look at me and say that again."

I gasped. My jaw fell into his hand as I openly gaped at him. He was grinning, just barely, but it was there.

"I almost kissed you tonight," I whispered. I knew he didn't have compulsion. Greyland only had one ability. There was nothing forcing me to do what he said, but I couldn't help it. I didn't recognize my voice. My eyes were glued to his as I felt my heart shatter and explode out of my chest.

He leaned closer. His breath was against my mouth, but he wasn't looking at me anymore. His gaze was locked on my lips. "I'm going to kiss you."

I couldn't find my voice. Couldn't move.

"Lilia." His gaze left my mouth for a second to meet mine. His hand trailed past my chin, cupping my neck instead. "Have you ever been kissed before?"

I shook my head which caused the pad of his thumb to dig into my throat.

"If you don't want me to kiss you, I need you to say something *right now*."

"It's just a dream," I whispered. "It's not real so it doesn't matter."

"It's as real as you want it to be," he breathed against my mouth.

He was hovering over me. I closed my eyes, wanting it, waiting for it—needing it. I could smell the faint taste of mint on his breath.

"Open your eyes."

They fluttered open. He still hadn't moved. His hand was half around my throat, half around the back of my neck while his other found my hip. My back was arched, and I hadn't realized my knees spread open until he slid between them.

"I want you looking at me when I kiss you," he murmured. "I want you to know it's *me* doing it."

Before I could react, his lips crashed into mine. I managed to keep my eyes open for two-three-four seconds before they closed on instinct, and I succumbed to the feeling that was Greyland Aaron Noren.

And I didn't just lose it, I exploded. I moved without thinking. My hands found his back, half pulling and half pushing him closer to me. I wanted to melt into this feeling, into him. I never wanted to stop kissing him. It was intoxicating, addicting.

I always envisioned my first kiss to be soft. A featherlight brush against the lips. Romantic and sensual. But this—I never imagined this. Never thought it could be like this.

We were all teeth and hands as we kept grabbing and pulling at each other, wanting to feel everything all at once.

I needed extra hands. I wanted them everywhere. I gripped his hair which was more coarse than I had imagined. I worked my way down his jawline, to his shoulders, over his stomach. I felt each indentation of his muscles flex beneath my touch. I kept moving against him, needing to be pressed together. I wasn't sure what parts of him I was brushing myself against. My only thought was that I wanted more.

He moaned as my lips parted, and his tongue found its way in my mouth the next heartbeat. Then I was moaning. Every sensation was running through me at once.

The taste of wine was still on his lips, and I realized that I still felt hazy from all the champagne I drank. Somehow I was still drunk when I fell asleep tonight, and it followed me in here.

I didn't care. It gave me courage. Made me want more and more.

He had pushed me down at some point. My back was resting against the cushions while he was still between my legs. If this wasn't a dream, I would have been mortified at the squeal I made as he ground his hips against mine.

I couldn't tell where his hands were. They kept moving, kept shifting, kept exploring. He had them all over me like he couldn't get enough. And whenever I felt like I couldn't handle the feeling of his hands, he would grind his hips against me, making sounds leave my mouth uncontrollably.

Then my shoulders were shaking.

"Fuck, Lilia. I've dreamt about this for so—"

Greyland's voice cut short as I woke up in a panic. My eyes fluttered open, and my vision focused on green ones. "What the hell are you dreaming about, Lilia?" Peter asked, mortified. His expression was a mixture of appall and disgust. "You're making weird noises."

I blinked slowly, trying to recall everything through the haze of alcohol as Peter's room shifted into view.

I kissed Greyland Noren.

I mean, it was only in my dreams, but I still dreamt that I kissed Greyland.

And it felt real.

"Take the sofa," my brother said, instantly drawing me back to reality. "I'm not sleeping with you while you're all weird."

I groaned, pushing Peter away. I could smell whiskey on his breath, and I wondered how late he was out partying and what time it was now.

Grabbing my pillow, I groggily made my way over to the sofa. But all I could think about was the green one from my dream and what I had just been doing on it.

I couldn't fall asleep again.

ELEVEN
GREYLAND

"Too bad Little isn't here to mend that," Lander teased as he sat down next to me. My ribs were bruised, and I had a cut running down my cheek, but I won my match so I didn't give a shit.

Two weeks had passed since my brother's wedding, and we were in Narway for the Six Battles. This town was probably my least favorite out of the six villages in Tennebris—with Backerly coming in at a close second—and I couldn't wait to go back to Kitlarn.

Narway was bland. There was nothing here but the school and rundown homes. They didn't even have a market. And beyond the lack of buildings, everything was flat. After the monorail passed the forest between Kitlarn and Palm, there were no trees, no mountains, no lakes—nothing.

Three menders I didn't care to learn the names of traveled with us, and I found myself searching for pale blonde hair even though I knew I wouldn't find any. Half of me was thankful Lilia wasn't here because if she was mending Lander I'd probably lose my shit.

Ever since Sie's wedding, I couldn't stop thinking about her and how she looked in that stupid green dress. Even worse, my mind kept replaying how she pushed me in the hallway. I had no idea why it was getting to me—all she did was shove me and told me she hates me, and I acted like she tried to kiss me...

Because I *wanted* her to kiss me. Because if Reagan hadn't walked in on us, I probably would have done it myself.

I tried to hook up with Falone last weekend, thinking I just needed to clear my head, but I couldn't go through with it. Every time I touched her, I kept thinking how she didn't feel like Lilia.

Now all I saw were her hazel eyes—in the trees, in the mud soaked grass, the main building outside of Narway, even their stupid guard uniforms were a mixture of her coloring.

"Why would I care?" I asked, watching Colton finish his match.

I could feel Lander grin at me even though I didn't look away from the fight. "You don't fool me, Noren. I've seen you staring at her these past two weeks."

"You're keeping tabs on me now?" I turned to look at him.

His eye was swollen shut, and his grin was bloody from his match. "Nah." He spit blood onto the dirt in front of my shoes. "I've only noticed because I've been staring at her too."

My spine straightened, and I tried to keep my face blank, but I couldn't. I knew Lander didn't really care about her. He was only doing it to get a rise out of me. Because he thought *I* cared.

"You can have her." I shrugged, then left the mender's tent.

"Maybe I will," he called after me as I walked off.

———

"Lilia Fervic and Lander Autions," Professor Jean called out. We were back in Abilities Class, and I'd seen Lilia go up against half our class so far, but I'd been dreading this.

I knew it was only a matter of time before my name was called next to hers, but I was scared shitless for what Lander would do when it was his turn. He wasn't allowed to compel her—but that wasn't why I was worried.

"Lander, use your power to project a weapon of your choice. Lilia, try to retrieve it from him."

Lander smiled. His golden markings flared to life as he immediately materialized a dagger. "Come and get it, Little," he taunted.

"No bodily harm," Professor Jean added. "I don't want to send anyone to the healers today."

Lander spun the blade in his hand as Lilia went into a fighting stance that was laughable. Considering she grew up with Peter, her capabilities of sparring didn't show. It pissed me off that he never bothered to train her. Of course, I didn't either. But the girl was weak. She had nothing going for her in a world where everyone was going to abuse her, and instead of helping prepare her, Peter acted like everything was fine and that his little sister wasn't one of the weakest Tennebrisians to ever exist.

I ground my teeth. I had no idea why it bothered me so much.

The only thing I could say about Lilia Fervic was that she was tenacious. She didn't give up, even when she should.

She made an offensive move on Lander who grinned as he stepped out of the way. Her silky blonde hair fell out of her braid, and she lost her footing and fell.

"Come on, you can do better than that." Lander teased, making a circle around her as she stood and straightened. She had her feet planted with her head turning to follow him, and I wanted to scream at her for being so stupid. You never planted your feet and you never let the person you're fighting get behind you. Goddess damn me, this was torture to watch.

Lander pushed her forward but not before I heard a rip in her shirt. She looked down at her blouse, attempting to grab the frayed ends. A mixture of disbelief and rage was written on her face.

"Oops. Was that the only shirt you could afford?"

She lunged at him again, just as clumsily and way too slow, exactly like the first time she tried. Anyone could see her coming. I was pretty sure one of the Tennebrisian penguins would have time to wobble out of the way. Her moves were too predictable. Hell, it looked like she was lunging in slow motion.

Another rip and Lilia's shirt was almost torn off of her. Her abdomen was fully exposed, and I caught a glimpse of her black bra.

My fists clamped at my sides as I called to my abilities. I knew Lander wasn't going to stop.

I cast my illusion into everyone in the room except Lander, Lilia, and… me. Just because I couldn't stop it, didn't mean everyone else had to see it.

Another tear and her shirt was falling to the floor. It was beyond ruined. Lander was probably right. I doubted she had another school uniform.

Everyone was still watching them spar, but to their eyes, her shirt was still on—ripped to pieces with a bit of her bra showing through just like it was when I started the illusion—and exactly how it was going to stay.

Her face reddened—half in anger, half in embarrassment.

Another move and Lander sliced the straps of her bra. I rolled my neck as I saw blood. He nicked her skin and it was on fucking purpose.

She gasped, grabbing hold of her shoulder where he cut her before she realized her bra was on the ground.

I tried not to look, but I was a dick and did anyway. Her boobs were fucking perfection, exactly how I imagined they'd be ever since I saw her in that green dress. I was going to kill Lander. I didn't want to have sex dreams about her—but holy fuck. I wasn't going to be able to get her out of my mind now.

Any arousal I felt immediately vanished as I noticed Lander was openly gawking too. "Who would have thought you'd have a nice, perky rack under all those clothes, Little."

Lilia was covering her chest with her hands but doing a fucking terrible job at it. *Just give up, Lil, go over to Grace, grab her blazer, and let Lander win.* I tried to will her into action, but the girl was stupidly stubborn.

I looked to Professor Jean. She wasn't stopping it. Maybe she would if she knew what was really happening. I let my illusion fade from her, and her brown eyes widened in horror as she realized Lilia was naked from the waist up.

"That's enough," Professor Jean finally called. "Lander wins. Lilia, cover yourself."

Lander winked as he walked over to me, but I kept staring at Lilia, waiting until she pulled her friend's blazer over her shoulders, and only then did I let my illusion drop from everyone else in the class.

TWELVE
LILIA

I WAS STILL FUMING after Abilities Class.

"How bad was it?" I asked Grace as we made our way toward the auditorium. The rest of our classes were canceled today for an official broadcast by the Council.

"Well, everyone knows you wear a black bra."

I was wearing one of Grace's uniforms, which was two sizes too small. It was obvious the blouse wasn't mine. Everyone would know Lander was right—I didn't have enough money for another outfit.

But Grace's words stopped me. Lander ruined my bra. My entire chest was on display for everyone to see. I was more worried if anyone saw my nipples, not my bra.

"Grace, I highly doubt seeing my bra was the worst of that."

Her golden hair whipped toward me. "What do you mean? What could have been worse?"

"My boobs were out," I whispered-yelled so no one else could hear.

"Lilia, I don't know if you and I were in the same class, but no one saw your boobs."

"Lander cut my bra—"

"He ruined your uniform, but he stopped at your shirt, Lil," she cut me off. "No one, and I mean no one, saw your boobs."

I frowned at her. I knew what happened. I was so embarrassed that I was certain I would still remember it centuries from now.

But then I remembered seeing Greyland. He was staring at me with such intensity that I completely forgot about Lander's knife for a split second.

It dawned on me then. He used his illusion. No one saw me half naked.

But that didn't mean *he* didn't see and somehow that felt worse than the entire class seeing. Why would he do that? Did he feel morally obligated since our brothers were friends?

"It's okay, Lilia," she added as we found our seats. "I highly doubt anyone will remember."

That was a lie. Even if it was only my bra, I could feel the constant stares I was getting from the guys in our class. I ignored it, but I still felt it. It didn't help that the shirt I was now wearing was skin tight, or the fact that every time I tried to tug it down, a sliver of my stomach was still showing.

The projector was pulled down across the stage, and our Principal was discussing something urgently with some of the professors.

"What do you think this is about?" I asked as Jaxson took the seat next to us.

"No idea," Grace whispered back. "But whatever it is can't be good. It wasn't a planned broadcast."

The screen flared to life, and Scotlind Noren flashed on the monitor. Only she looked different from when I last saw her, such a stark contrast from how beautiful she was in her wedding dress.

Now she wore a gray dress. It was simple, plain, nothing like a future queen would wear. But it wasn't the dress that had my mouth gaping open, it was *her*. She'd lost weight and it had only been three weeks since their wedding. I could see her ribs jutting through the thin material, and her wrists were bruised beneath... beneath...

I swallowed.

She was wearing shackles.

A guy was standing next to her. He was sweating profusely, his clothes completely drenched, but I kept staring at the princess. She looked calm. Enraged, but calm.

The cameras shifted, and I finally saw the rest of the room—I took a guess it was the throne room. It looked similar to their wedding ceremony, just not as garnished.

King Lunder was standing on a raised dais with two more Tennebrisians behind him. One of them gestured to someone off screen, and the next second, the cameras panned to Sie as he walked toward them.

My breathing hitched as I started hyperventilating. What could have happened in three weeks to change things this much?

I looked away from the monitor, and I immediately spotted Greyland. He was staring at the screen. His mouth slightly hung open—whatever we were about to witness, he had no idea either.

"Good evening, fellow Tennebrisians," King Lunder said, immediately quieting the crowd gathered inside the throne room. "Thank you for tuning in today for this mandatory announcement. It displeases me as to why we are meeting today. Our princess has betrayed and deceived us all. We call her forward today to speak the truth as to why our prince has been absent recently."

He gestured to where Scotlind stood chained. Her bright blue eyes seemed to be the only thing about her that still held color. She didn't say anything, but I could tell there was a living storm under her.

The cameras didn't shift away from her, and I waited for what would happen next. It felt like minutes before they finally panned back to the dais.

I caught a glimpse of Sie before the cameras shifted again. His jaw ticked as he looked down at her, but then it was gone. A mask of cool indifference stood in its place, and I knew it was something all the Norens had mastered.

Another Council member stepped forward. His hair had a thin layer of grease to it that I was certain even a bath wouldn't fix. And there was something about him that felt wrong. "Your princess has betrayed our prince and, in turn, our Kingdom. She has been having an affair with this male." A few gasps echoed across the throne room from those in attendance. "Some of you may recognize him as a former ranking evaluator. Many Tennebrisians were confused as to why a rank zero was selected for our prince. To be honest, the Council felt that having a zero on the throne would be a good thing. At the time, we hoped to separate the divide and rift that has been growing amongst our ranking system, but Scotlind has proven us otherwise. It has been discovered that Joshuan Carithin," the Council member pointed to the male, "has been working with Scotlind from the beginning to tamper with her results in order for her to be selected as the princess.

"Our system was designed to help our people thrive. It is needed in order to keep things fair, to keep things functioning. If our society doesn't abide by their Trial outcomes, everything will go into chaos. Which was exactly the motive that Scotlind and Joshuan were seeking. They wanted to overthrow the system, the Council, and Prince Noren himself.

"It is made clear now that a rank zero will stop at nothing to get what they desire. The greediness amongst the lower ranks is amplifying, and as such, we will be investigating the ranking system further after this incident. A rank zero will stop at nothing to move up in our society, and we simply cannot allow them to do so. We will be working closely with King Arcane Xandrin of Lux to look into modeling our system more closely to theirs. More will be coming in the next couple of weeks about what to expect. But many changes will be made in order to protect ourselves from something like this ever happening again."

I stopped breathing. I could barely focus on what was being said. They are going to make changes in Tennebris, but it wasn't in favor of rank zeroes. At some point Grace had grabbed my hand. She was squeezing it so hard, but I barely noticed.

I was numb.

This couldn't be happening. From everything Peter told me about her, this couldn't be true. There was no way.

"Do you admit to these charges, Scotlind Rumor?"

The cameras focused on her again. She was trembling now.

My own breathing hitched. I could tell she was struggling. It looked like she was fighting as her entire body started to shake. Her teeth gritted as she whispered, "Yes."

Scotlind paled after she said it. Her face drained of color. She went to open her mouth again, but as soon as she did, someone strapped a gag over her, stopping her words. Tears pooled down her cheeks, blurring her freckles and I knew... I just knew...

"She's being compelled."

"What?" Jaxson turned toward me. So did about five other people around us. I hadn't realized I said it out loud.

I lowered my voice. "How can anyone believe this?"

The screen flashed to my brother, and my heart sank. Peter was there, but he wasn't stopping it. He told me she was his friend.

At some point, they dragged Scotlind up onto the dais with Sie, and we all watched as they annulled their marriage.

When the broadcast ended and the monitor went out, our Principal stepped forward. "As King Lunder and Synder have made abundantly clear, there will be a lot of changes coming from the Council over the next couple of weeks. We will keep you all informed as we launch into navigating the changes required to mimic Luxian structure."

———

Two weeks later we were told there was another announcement. We were in the auditorium again, and I was terrified about what else could go wrong.

King Lunder and Synder continued to spin their lies about rank zeroes, with their main focus being how closely related to humans they thought they were. It was bullshit. Any rank zero that wasn't declared a servant during their Trials now were. Many were ripped from their homes. It didn't matter if they had a family or another low level job they were good at, all zeroes were servants now. Before it was *most*—eighty percent of zeroes ended up in the role. I knew because I was scared. I had spent countless nights studying the outcomes of Trials to see if I stood a chance in cooking or mending. I became obsessive.

But now all that hope was gone. Me taking all those extra classes would result in nothing if I came out without abilities during my rank evaluation.

I couldn't stomach hearing how terrible everyone thought zeroes were. I didn't want to listen to it. I had hoped going into this year that Scotlind Rumor would change things for us, and I guess in a way she did. It just wasn't how I thought it would go. Everything was all wrong.

I knew it wasn't Scotlind's fault. I could see through it. It was a setup. She was a rank zero. Her actions weren't her own. If she was my brother's friend, then I believed her. Peter had the best judgment of character out of anyone I knew. I swore half the time it was an ability of his. So if Peter liked Scotlind and still saw the good in her, then I would too.

Except I hadn't seen my brother since he appeared on that broadcast, and the last time I saw him in person was at their wedding.

I hadn't been able to go home since coming to school—I never could. My only way to get back to town was to ask Greyland for a ride, which I wasn't about to do.

But before I left for school, Peter said he'd visit by now. He promised me he'd stop by Kitlarn. He did every year since he graduated, always forcing Sie to drive him here, and Sie never complained because he'd do anything for Peter, even if it meant coming back home to see me.

He promised me things wouldn't change since Sie won the King's Tournament. He told me he'd come half way to Yule and then again for the holiday. But it was way past halfway to Yule. He should have been here by now.

I tried not to worry, but I couldn't help it. What if something happened after that first broadcast with Scotlind? What if he was dragged down with her? Surely Sie would have said something by now if he had been. Right?

My breath was in my chest as I waited for the broadcast to start with Grace. I kept praying to Pylemo that the announcement didn't involve Sie naming a new second… It couldn't be about Peter.

But as soon as the broadcast started, I realized I wasn't prepared for what it was actually about.

Synder came onto the screen. His face had a constant shimmer of oil, and his hair looked so greasy I couldn't tell if it was by choice.

We'd been seeing a lot of him—this was the fifth broadcast since they annulled Sie's marriage—and after the third one, I learned he was the current second.

In all honesty, I should have already known who he was. Broadcasts weren't uncommon—though this was a record high for how many were airing in a two week span. I just hated politics and usually zoned out during them. But not anymore. Now, I'd been soaking in every lie the two of them were spilling.

Only this time, Synder was alone. He wasn't being aired alongside the king.

"My fellow Tennebrisians, it brings me grave despair to share the news I have today."

Please don't be about Peter. Please don't be about Peter.

"King Lunder is dead."

A gasp rang out inside the auditorium, and although we were only watching from a screen, Synder took a pause, like he knew the reaction his words would cause. I could barely focus on what he was saying, couldn't register his voice as he briefed us on how the king died.

It all felt too wrong.

"I will be your king while Sie Noren continues to transition into the role. Once he is crowned, I will step down—" My heart relaxed a fraction. He didn't mention anything about Peter. So that meant he was fine, right? "—that being said, there is much to discuss. I will personally be looking into the current situation with rank zeroes," Synder continued. "As of now, everyone who has already had their

Trials has transitioned into the role of a servant. There will be another broadcast in a week. I need some time to go over all the necessary changes we still need to make, but mark my words, Tennebris will thrive. Never again will our society be manipulated by the greed of the lower class. We will see to it that structure is at the forefront of importance..."

Grace grabbed onto my hand, and I tried not to cry. They still weren't done with their changes. But what more could they possibly do? Zeroes were already all servants.

I focused on my breathing, trying not to break down in front of everyone.

"Are you okay?" Grace asked. I hadn't even realized the broadcast ended, and everyone started getting out of their seats.

I nodded. "I'll meet you in our dorm. There's something I have to do first."

I didn't wait to see her reaction as I ran out of the building to find Greyland Noren.

———

"GREYLAND," I called after him. He stopped but didn't turn around. He was with all three of his friends, about to enter Hiwet Hall where I couldn't follow.

"What do you want, Little?" Lander asked. His brown eyes looked me up and down, pausing over my shirt. I was still wearing Grace's uniform, and every time I saw him, I felt like he could see through it.

I glared but didn't acknowledge him, instead I focused on Greyland. "I need to talk with you. *Alone.*"

"Whatever you wanna tell him, you can say in front of us." Lander smirked.

All four of them were facing me now, and I tried not to balk. Even though I'd deny it to the Goddesses, they were all intimidating.

Colton was the tallest, but I wasn't sure if it was only his afro making him seem taller. I didn't completely hate him. Besides making inappropriate jokes, he wasn't all bad. Mack was the only one I could fully stand. When he was alone, without his friends, he was actually nice.

It was only Lander and Greyland who were tied for being the biggest jerks.

I hated it.

I couldn't understand how people who looked so beautiful on the outside could be so rotten on the inside. All four of them were attractive and all predicted to be strong during their Trials. If the Six Battles were any indication, each of them would make a name for themselves.

Lander ran his fingers through his curls. "Unless you want to talk privately in our suite, *Little*? I wouldn't mind seeing more of you again—"

"I'll be back," Greyland gritted out as he started stalking toward me. It took me a second to register that he was actually agreeing to talk with me. By the time I realized it, he had already passed me, and I had to practically run to catch up.

"Can you slow down?" I called, my breath collecting in a puff of air in front of me. It was starting to transition from summer to winter. The air was shifting, drawing slightly colder, and the sky was darkening more and more every day.

Greyland whirled. He looked so—pissed off and on edge. "What do you want, Lilia?"

I exhaled, preparing myself for my question. "Have you heard from your brother?"

His dark brows furrowed like my question took him off guard. Maybe it did. I had never, ever asked to talk to him during school before. "No. Why?"

I started tucking my hair behind my ear, even though the strands wouldn't stay and kept falling over my face. The wind wasn't helping either.

"I just... I haven't heard from Peter. He usually visits by now and..." I let my voice trail off. I was terrified of the changes happening at the castle and even more terrified for my brother.

He frowned for a second, and I felt the full weight of his scowl.

"I'm going home next weekend. I'll ask my mom if she's heard anything."

"Thank you."

He nodded, started to walk away, then stopped. "Lilia?"

"Yes?" I breathed.

"Don't ever come to my dorm again. If you want to talk to me, find some other way."

THIRTEEN
GREYLAND

"Sie, what are you doing here?" I asked. My brother was standing in the middle of the foyer in our family home. I took the weekend to drive home. I heard my father was going to be out of the house, plus I missed my mom and wanted to see her. I usually tried to visit once a month, and I promised Lilia I'd ask about Peter. I just hadn't expected to see my brother.

I did a quick scan of his body. He looked like he was on the brink of death or, at least, on the verge of passing out. "What's wrong? Are you okay?"

"I'm fine." He attempted to smile, but I saw right through it. He was shaking profusely, and his abnormally pale skin looked sickly.

Our mother came into the foyer and halted as if she'd seen a ghost. "I wasn't aware you were coming home today. No one notified us of your visit," she said as she started shooing the servants away.

"They wouldn't." Sie leaned against a pillar, and as much as he tried playing the gesture off as casual, I knew he was leaning because he had to—he couldn't stand up straight. "The Council doesn't know I'm here. I didn't use the monorail."

"You teleported all the way here?" I gasped.

He nodded but didn't elaborate any further.

"Why?" Mother asked, scanning Sie from head to toe.

"I wanted to see my brother," was all he answered, but I felt him enter my mind at the same time, *I need to talk to you in private.*

I smiled, not wanting to give anything away to our mother. She knew Sie talked to me in my mind, and if she thought we were now, she'd never leave us alone. "Come on, let's go to my room. I'll get you some water."

Our mother looked between us. She was hesitant, even if she over-compensated and acted like she wasn't. She wanted to say more, but she always walked on thin ice with Sie. "Fine, but you will stay for dinner. I'll have the servants prepare your favorite."

It wasn't a question—I guess that meant we were having beef tonight. Sie kicked off the pillar and walked toward her, gently kissing her on the cheek. "Yes, mother," he said before following me up the stairs.

As soon as I locked my bedroom door, I whirled on him. I assumed Sie was going to be a wreck from whatever happened between him and Scotlind. It was obvious my brother loved the girl, and I could see through his mask of indifference during their annulment. But I never expected him to be this bad, this bent out of shape over her... "What's going on? You don't look well."

He shook his head, grabbing my wrist. "Not here." His skin felt clammy and freezing at the same time. I went to respond, but he tele-ported us out of the house before I even had time to open my mouth.

Sie barely landed before he jumped again, each time not giving me a second to take in where we were going. I knew we were outside. I could glimpse trees and bark before everything became a blur again.

Six jumps later, he finally let me go, and I threw up the moment we landed. I hated my brother's teleportation—I mean, it was cool as shit, and I was envious of it—but my stomach never agreed with the jostling.

I wiped my mouth on the back of my sleeve. "I forgot how much teleporting sucks," I said before I looked over at my brother. He was vomiting right alongside me. His ability never affected him, no matter how many times I'd seen him jump, he never once got sick. "Shit, Sie, what's going on?"

"I had to speak with you without anyone overhearing," he managed to get out.

I did a quick once over of our surroundings. We were somewhere between Kitlarn and Palm based on the woods, and we were standing outside a run-down cabin, but I quickly turned my attention back on my brother.

He was leaning heavily against some of the wooden flanks, about to collapse. "Are you ill?"

He shook his head.

"Then what's wrong because you look like you're on the brink of death, and you're scaring me."

"I'm fine, Grey—"

"No, you aren't," I cut him off. I was sick of the bullshit, sick of him hiding things from me because he was trying to protect me. If something was wrong, I needed to know. "You're acting weird, and you're so pale you look like a ghost. Not to mention you haven't stopped shaking or sweating since you arrived. And you lost weight."

"Let's go inside, and I'll tell you everything." He managed to stand upright.

"The hunting cabin," I murmured when I finally realized where he brought me. "I forgot about this place." I grinned, remembering all the times I begged Sie and Peter to bring me with them when they came here. I loved spending time with them, even if they tried to avoid me like the plague at times. But it was an excuse to leave our shit-show of a house, an excuse to get away from our dad, and it was the only time I got to be with my brother without all the stressors our father placed on him. "You fixed it up."

In truth, it still looked like a rotting cabin, but compared to the memories I last had of it, it was a huge improvement. There were no longer holes in the wood, and the door actually stayed shut.

He nodded his head, then pushed the door open, almost falling inside from the momentum. Multiple bedrolls lined the far corner of the room, chopped wood was neatly stacked by the fireplace, buckets of fresh water were along the other wall, and some canned food was stacked next to it that wouldn't expire for a long time.

I strode over to the fireplace. "I'll start a fire, but you better start talking now, starting with what's wrong with you."

My brother collapsed onto one of the new chairs that now flanked the room. "I've been taking poison every day."

"Why?" I asked as I threw another log into the fireplace, trying my damned best to remain calm. I focused on getting it started because my brother felt like he was seconds away from freezing to death. His skin had never been that cold before...

"Because King Lunder was murdered."

I turned to face him just as the pile of wood burst into flames. "But I thought he died eating—"

"No. He was *murdered*."

"By who?" I asked. I knew the king had died. Synder announced it during the last broadcast, but for Sie to admit it was intentional...

If it wasn't for Peter telling me that there was an attack made on Scotlind prior to their wedding, I probably would have believed what the Council was shoving down our throats.

But I knew Sie better than anyone. He loved her and whatever was going on, he wasn't part of it.

This was the first time I was even getting a chance to see him since everything went down. I wasn't brought to the castle for their annulment, and I had to find out at the same time as everyone else in the auditorium in Kitlarn.

"Synder, I'm certain of it," he answered. "And I think he's trying to take me out too."

He filled me in on everything that had happened since their wedding. My gut rutted as I thought of him being tortured for days in a warehouse while I had no idea. He almost died, while I was what, competing in the Six Battles and taking classes? Kitlarn felt like a joke compared to what was happening to my brother—what Scotlind and him went through. And I knew what he was telling me was a watered down version of it. I knew what he went through was worse.

It shouldn't have surprised me that the Council was lying to us. In the back of my mind, I already had my suspicions. But I was still shocked as hell when Sie told me they sent Scotlind to Lux and told our people she had an affair.

I still couldn't believe she was Luxian. Sie had to tell me five times before it finally sunk in. But it confirmed everything was a setup. They were manipulating her to make changes in our society. I just didn't know how far they would go.

"Do you remember Moli?" Sie asked, pulling me from my thoughts. I was sitting down at the table with him, my back facing the fire, and had no idea why he was asking me that.

"The healer that was assigned to you growing up?" I briefly remembered having one at our house, but ever since Sie moved out after graduating and finishing his Trials, we didn't need one. I hadn't seen the girl for nearly four years.

"Yeah, she's at the castle with me. She's the one who told me how Lunder was murdered, and she's been giving me the poison every day."

"There's no lasting side effects that could hurt you, right?"

"No," he said too quickly that there was a fat chance I was believing him. Just looking at him right now told me everything I needed to know. But I also knew him well enough to know this was the end of our conversation.

"I'm going to be fine," he added, clearly for my benefit, because he also knew me better. "My body just needs a couple more days to adjust. That's all. But that's not the reason I needed to talk with you. Do you remember how to get here on foot?"

"Yeah, I think so."

"I need to know for sure, Grey. I can mark some trees for a path for you, but that leaves this place vulnerable to being tracked."

The seriousness to his tone had me sitting up straighter. "I can get here on my own."

"Okay, good. Because if anything happens to me, I need you to bring Mom here. Take Lilia and Peter's parents too. Don't wait, don't hesitate. The moment you suspect anything, you leave everything behind, and you come here. Tell no one about it."

"Sie, you're scaring me." I could feel tears prick the back of my eyes, but I refused to shed any. If Sie could be strong about this, so could I. "If things are really bad at the castle, if you think they're trying to kill you for the throne, you need to step down."

"I can't."

"Yes, you can. Nothing is worth your life, not even being the king."

"It's not about being king," he snapped.

"Then what? Is it Father? Because we will deal with him together." Rage was festering in me now. Sie was stubborn to a fault, but I couldn't grasp why he was putting himself through this. Growing up he always took the brunt of our dad's anger to spare me—but this—I didn't get it, couldn't wrap my head around why he was staying in a place where people were actively trying to kill him.

"Grey, stop," he said gently. And fuck, if I thought I wasn't crying, but I couldn't lose my brother... I just couldn't. "It's not about Dad," he added.

"Then what? Because I don't understand what's so important that you're willing to go through all of this for? Come home, please, brother."

"It's her."

I was silent for way too long, but I had no idea what to say back to that. If she was already handed over to the Lux King, there was nothing my brother could do about it. I saw the Luxian ruler at their wedding, and the man looked intimidating as hell.

"You can't get her back. She's gone, Sie. She's—"

"I know, Grey," he yelled, cutting me off. "I don't need you reminding me that she's gone and that I've fucked the only good thing in my life, and the chances of me getting her back are slim to none. I fucking know."

"Okay," I said. I'd never seen my brother so distraught, so desperate for something. "If you think she's worth all of this, I'll stand by you, but I don't like it." I paused. "Promise me that you'll fight back. Promise me you'll win."

"Thank you." He reached over the table and clamped his sweaty palm over mine. "And I promise."

I leaned back in my chair once Sie pulled away. "Is Peter still in Lux looking for Scottie?"

"Yeah."

"Okay." I nodded. "Lilia has been going crazy. He didn't tell her he was going, and she's been worried sick, thinking the worst."

"I know. I'm sorry for that. I haven't been able to come here until today, and Peter didn't have time to warn her. Everything happened so fast. How is Lilia?"

"She's managing as best as she can… no help from me," I murmured under my breath. Managing was an understatement. "She pretends she's doing fine and completely ignores the fact that everyone knows she's going to be a zero." I took a breath, preparing myself for my next question. "I heard rumors that they're thinking of forcing everyone to go through some sort of compulsion. Is that true? Are they really trying to do that?"

"It is," Sie said. "I know, it's fucked. Synder wants to find out who is a zero right away and not let them have an education. Since only an unranked Tennebrisian can be compelled, he's trying to pass a law that would make compulsion a requirement to get into school. It hasn't happened yet, but there is a chance that it might."

"That's messed up." I ran my hand over my face. "Everything's going to shit."

Mack was right about what he'd overheard and if that actually happened—I had no idea what I was going to do to help Lilia. I wasn't delusional into thinking I could actually make a difference.

"I know, Grey," was all my brother said, because what else could he say? Everything was fucked.

FOURTEEN
LILIA

"YOU KNOW, I wanted to ask you to take me home with you."

"Why didn't you?" We were sitting on the sofa together. I was wearing one of Grace's t-shirts to bed and it followed me into my dream. Greyland frowned. "I would have driven you."

I rolled my eyes and gently kicked his thigh under the blanket. "Yeah because that would have gone over well. Dream you, yes, you would have driven me in a heartbeat, but the real you? Not a chance."

He frowned again. "I've driven you to and from school before, Lilia."

"Yeah when it's necessary and because our mothers arranged it, not because I asked or you felt like being nice all of a sudden."

"I never knew you wanted to go home during school."

"I always do. I mean, as much as I love having some electricity and running water in the dorms, I miss my parents when I'm here. I just don't have the money to take public transportation home."

I didn't bother asking Dream-Greyland about Peter. He wouldn't actually know. This wasn't the real him. So I bit down the question burning inside me and tried to focus on anything else instead, which resulted in me wondering how Greyland actually slept—in my dream he was in sweats and a loose shirt.

His fingers started absentmindedly trailing up and down my bare leg. "I'm sorry."

I looked up at him and found his dark eyes already assessing me. My foot was resting against his leg, and I fought a shiver as his fingers grazed my thigh before going back down again. "You're not actually sorry."

"Why do you always do that?"

"Do what?"

"Don't believe me when I tell you something."

My brows furrowed. "Because you're my subconscious. You're everything I want you to be, but actually not."

He grabbed my leg then, his hand trailing up my hip as he pulled me on top of him. It was a position we kept finding ourselves in ever since the wedding. Now that I started kissing Greyland Noren in my dreams, I couldn't stop. He was addicting. I always woke up craving more and found myself staring at his lips in real life. Ever since the wedding, it was like the pin in the grenade was gone, and every time we saw each other now, we exploded. Usually, it would only take us five minutes into my dream before one of us was on top of the other. Tonight was probably the longest we made it talking before I was kissing him.

"I'll be anything you tell me to be, Lilia Fervic." His breath hit my cheek. I was always so surprised that I could smell the mint from it like he'd just brushed them before finding me in my dreams.

"Then. Be." I pressed my lips to his, speaking into his mouth, "Mine."

"Done." His hand found its way behind my neck as he wrapped his fingers into my hair—something he did often. I was sitting on his lap now, my body flush against his, save for my hand resting on his chest.

He turned us, pushing us both onto our sides against the couch, and my legs instantly wrapped around his.

"I want this to be real," I said in between kisses. I couldn't hide the confliction I felt every time I was happy with him in my dreams. It was perfect, too perfect, but when I woke up every morning, Greyland

Noren was everything I hated, and I was once again reminded of what this was.

"This is real for me," he whispered so softly I thought I imagined it.

I kept kissing him. He wouldn't understand. He wasn't real, but if this version of him was all I got, then I'd take it.

Even if it'd only ever be a dream.

———

THE FOLLOWING WEEK, classes were canceled first thing Monday morning. I didn't get a chance to ask Greyland—*the real Greyland*—if he talked to his mom about Peter, and I had no idea how I was going to since he told me I couldn't go to his dorm.

But as I sat down in between Jaxson and Grace for yet another broadcast, I realized I had bigger issues.

"What is that?" Jaxson asked.

I didn't answer. I couldn't find my voice even if I wanted to because the stage had a boiling iron cauldron with only one poker sticking out of the flames. A few members of the High Council were on the stage with our Principal, alongside a couple dozen Tennebrisian Guards.

Our Principal stepped forward. "We have received orders from King Synder. As of today, rank zeroes will no longer be taking classes."

A gasp rang out among our classmates. I sank back into my seat, unable to breathe.

"Starting at the age of six, every Tennebrisian will undergo compulsion. Anyone that can fight the compulsion is ranked and will receive an education. Anyone that can't will automatically become a servant."

I knew my eyes were brimming with tears because I couldn't see. Everything was blurry. The only thing I could focus on were his words. They were going to pull us all out of school...

"Since this is a new process, we recognize the need to take these changes slowly. As of today, anyone that is found to be a zero won't be taking classes. Since we already know they will become servants, they don't need an education to prepare for Trials. It's a waste of resources—"

"Waste of resources," I found myself repeating the words on a whispered breath, but I felt like a corpse. I couldn't blink. I knew if I did I'd be able to see again, but then that would mean my tears would fall, and I wasn't ready...

"We're implementing this new law immediately. All upcoming prospective six year olds will undergo compulsion, as well as every student already in school. As for every zero currently enrolled, King Synder has developed a Student-Servant program to help ease the transition, but I'll get more into that later."

He clapped his hands together, and the noise was so jostling against the silent auditorium that I jumped, and my tears finally spilled onto my cheeks. With that, everything came into focus again.

"Let's start the Branding Ceremony. It will be quick and straight-forward. A simple compulsion and we'll know who has abilities."

"They can't do this," Grace whispered at my side.

But they could, and they were...

And they wanted to do this to six year olds.

I'd never been compelled before. I knew it would have immediately told me if I had powers. Peter had asked me if I wanted to be compelled when I was ten. It would have given me my answer. I would have immediately known if I was a zero, but I couldn't do it. I think I wasn't ready. I was too much of a coward to find out, but now I didn't have a choice, and I was going to find out in front of everyone...

"What the fuck?" Jaxson swore. "They have a knife."

I looked up toward the stage. Guards started bringing the first row up.

My breath left me as I saw Alec step forward and hand a knife off to one of my classmates. He was the guy who had asked me to dance at the wedding, the same Advenian that Greyland later told me would compel zeroes to sleep with him.

"Cut your arm," he compelled.

The knife didn't move.

"You can go back to your seat," our Principal said.

I waited and watched as classmate after classmate took the knife. Thirteen people had taken their seats so far. Thirteen people had abilities, but now...

A scream echoed across the walls as a girl dragged the knife across her forearm. Blood dripped onto the floor and two guards immediately stepped forward to grab her shoulders. Her screams continued as they held out her left wrist and another guard grabbed the poker from the iron cauldron. They were branding her *now*...

I started shaking. Maybe I was going into shock. I heard more screams. Saw more blood. Watched as the iron poker went in and out of the fire. More people who were zeroes were getting branded.

There were thirty now, and they weren't allowed to sit back down. They stood there, toward the back of the stage, and waited.

I watched as Greyland and his friends walked up on stage. Grey was quiet. His head flicked over the zeroes standing in the back before he grabbed the knife from Alec. He knew he had powers, but Alec still sent the compulsion to him. One second he was holding the knife, the next he was passing it back, unharmed.

Grace gently grabbed my arm when our row was called. I stared at Jaxson's short hair as he walked in front of me. I couldn't breathe as he passed the knife back to Alec and then it was my turn.

Alec grinned down at me. "Lilia." He met me halfway, leaning down as he gently placed the knife in my hand.

It hadn't been cleaned.

A metallic tang hit my nostrils, and I realized I was standing in a puddle of blood. The hem of my gray pants were slowly becoming drenched.

The knife in my hand felt so heavy. I wanted to drop it. I wanted to run away.

"Cut your arm, Lilia Fervic." The compulsion rang through me. Alec's voice was soft, light, almost musical. My hand was shaking as it lifted on its own accord. I watched in horror as I dragged it from the nook of my elbow all the way down to my wrist. A scream wrenched from my voice—I couldn't tell if it was from pain or shock—*I shouldn't have been shocked.* In the back of my mind, I always knew. I never manifested any abilities.

I was surprised by how much blood I was losing. I could see my muscle beneath the liquid pouring out. For a moment, I just stood there, gaping at my arm, stunned at how much red I was seeing. I didn't mean to press the blade so deep into my skin. I didn't mean to cut myself at all. I didn't want to.

I glanced up at Alec, his brown eyes were assessing. He had a coy grin on his face as he stepped forward before gently grabbing the knife from my hand.

"I'll put a good word in for you once you graduate. I'm in need of a servant in Palm," he whispered. I was certain no one else heard, but it felt like I was being yelled at. I kept hearing his voice over and over again in my mind.

Servant. Servant. Servant.

Before I could respond, I was yanked backward. Hands gripped my shoulders, and I was half dragged in front of the cauldron. Another guard grabbed my wrist—the same one that was bleeding and already writhing in agony. They pulled my arm down, extending it until my skin was exposed.

I glanced up then. I was facing the auditorium. Everyone was staring, watching how we all reacted. I knew tears were falling down my face, but I couldn't feel them anymore.

Dark eyes immediately caught my focus. Greyland was standing. His fists were clenched at his sides as he watched and he looked—

I screamed again as the iron clamped over my wrist. A burning sensation seared through me. It made the cut explode with pain as the hot coal pressed directly over it.

Then it was over. The burning faded to a dull throb, my cut still stung, but the iron was removed, and I was thrown toward the back of the stage.

I was a rank zero.

FIFTEEN
GREYLAND

SIE WAS RIGHT. He warned me over the weekend that he thought something like this might happen. I just didn't think it would be so soon.

It was barbaric. The amount of blood on the stage was concerning, but they didn't call in the school's Luxian healer. Hell, they didn't even have a Tennebrisian mender. They wanted to make a point and it was working. They didn't care about the students forced to stand on the stage, and they weren't going to heal them.

Mack tugged me back down into my seat after Lilia went up. I honestly hadn't realized I stood.

"Are you okay?" he whispered.

I couldn't answer. My throat had a lump in it preventing me from using it, and my tongue felt like sandpaper. I saw Alec whisper something to her. Her hazel eyes widened at whatever he said. I was seconds away from going up onto the stage and punching him.

I rolled my neck. "I'm fine," I lied.

My brother needed to come to power *now*, but his coronation was still too far away. I knew there was more he wasn't telling me. Sie had a habit of keeping me in the dark. He didn't want to worry me and instead took the brunt of whatever was happening full on. He did it all the time growing up, but I wasn't a child anymore.

Lander grinned on the other side of Mack. "It's about time something like this happened."

I had to fight my composure as they went through the remaining students. By the end of it, forty-two were rank zeroes. Forty-two of us were now branded and wouldn't get a Trial.

Principal Asfon came back to the stage. They still hadn't cleared any of the blood, and his boots splashed in it as he stepped in front of the microphone. There were hundreds of red tracks starting from the center of the stage toward the back.

The Kitlarn auditorium was abnormally bright. It was the only place in the Academy that didn't have any windows or fireplaces, and because of it, it was brimming with electricity. It was the only similarity all six schools had because it was required for broadcasts. Even the poor schools like Narway and LakeWood had an electric auditorium provided by the Council.

The projector worked on some sort of pulley rope. It could go up and down depending on if they needed to air anything. Right now, it was up, and all the lights were turned on, illuminating everything happening in grotesque detail.

Lilia was still standing at the back of the stage. She'd stopped crying now, but her eyes were swollen as she cradled her arm and the front of her uniform was soaked in blood.

"As I mentioned before, this is a transitional phase for us. King Synder has developed a program within the six schools to ease rank zeroes into our society. Instead of placing them into jobs right away, they will serve the school until it's their time to graduate. Each year will have their own set of servants. Here are yours." He gestured toward our classmates at his back. Lilia stiffened, her gaze finally looked up from her mangled arm.

"There will be an opportunity for any ranked student that wants a personal servant on campus to acquire one. We will host a Bidding Ceremony for the forty-two servants in your year.

"If there are no bids placed on a rank zero, then they will be a servant to the school itself, and I will see to their tasks. However, if anyone is interested in a servant, you can bid amongst yourselves to claim one. Whoever has the highest bids will get the servant for the remainder of the year. Since you are in your twelfth year, this will be the only time to bid. As for the lower classes, the start of each school year will host the Bidding Ceremony so rank zeroes have opportunities to serve and learn from different people.

"The servants will be at your disposal and whatever funds made on the bid will go toward the school itself. The rank zeroes will serve on a similar schedule to your classes. They are yours to order during the week, and they may be provided with weekends off."

"Fuck yes." Lander grinned. I saw him lean forward in his seat, his eyes on Lilia.

"Since we are already well into your school year, we are going to start your Bidding Ceremony today. For now, rank zeroes may keep the dorms they have been assigned to. Moving forward, we will be building separate dorm quarters for zeroes from the money the school earns off the bids. That being said, if any ranked Tennebrisian has an issue continuing to room with a zero, please find me, and I'll see what I can do."

Mack nudged my arm. I looked down and saw my hands were white. I was gripping the armrest to the chair like my life depended on it. I let go, flexing my fingers, and tried to breathe in and out through my nose.

"Let's start the Bidding Ceremony," Principal Asfon called. Someone came onto the stage—I noticed the abnormally bright colored eyes and knew they were Luxian. I exhaled, relieved that they at least got a healer, and Lilia's arm would stop bleeding—

"Each Bidding Ceremony will use the assistance of a Luxian *Alluse* user. We don't want anyone to win a bid using any abilities, so he is here to temporarily put a stop to your powers."

Alluse user, not healer.

Immediately my abilities vanished. I'd never had my powers

suppressed before, and I hated the feeling. It felt wrong, like they were taking away a piece of my existence.

"Your year has forty-two rank zeroes, which means a potential of forty-two bids. We will go one at a time by their last names." A teacher passed Principal Asfon a piece of paper. I guess they were recording the students who cut themselves. "Okay." He unfolded the paper. "Starting with Kiti Aviels. Do we have any bids?"

I watched in horror as our classmates fought over her. The girl was shaking, audibly sobbing, but I didn't give her more than two seconds of my attention. I kept staring at Lilia. She must have felt it because her gaze flicked to mine.

Three more students were bought. One had no bids and was going to Principal Asfon. Then her name was called.

"Lilia Fervic."

Shit. My family had money. I could bid on her if it meant no one else getting their hands on her, but I'd be in for a beating once my dad found out.

I watched as the first round of bids went out. More people wanted her than the others—probably because of her brother's status—no, that wasn't true. It was because she was Goddess-damn gorgeous and all these fuckers wanted to take advantage of her.

Then Lander started bidding.

Fuck it. I didn't care. My dad could do whatever the hell he wanted to me as long as Lander couldn't do whatever he wanted to her.

"One hundred knell," I called. I didn't recognize my voice.

Everyone stilled. It was the highest amount that was thrown out so far. "Well, that is a generous contribution, thank you, Mr. Noren."

"Two hundred knell," Lander called. I glanced at him past Mack. He was smirking, his leg propped against his knee.

"Two-fifty."

"Three hundred." Grace stood from across the room. I turned to look at her, she had tears running down her face as her head whipped from Lander, to me, to Lilia up on the stage.

I should let her go to Grace. It was the reasonable thing to do. She'd treat Lilia the best—

"Four," Lander called. His leg was down now, and he was leaning forward in his seat. "I can go all day, Kilena." He smirked at Grace.

I ground my jaw. I was going to get the living shit beaten out of me. "One thousand."

I waited for Lander or Grace to reply. I knew Lander's family had money, not nearly as much as mine, but he could afford to go higher if he wanted.

Lilia's gaze widened, her head kept flicking back and forth between us. I didn't have time to worry about what she made of it. There was no way I was letting her go to Lander, and if Grace couldn't match my bid, then that was her problem.

"One thousand, one hundred," Lander drawled. He wasn't smirking anymore, but I knew he wasn't backing down.

"Sold. Lilia Fervic is now owned by Lander Autions."

"Fuck no," I raised my voice at the same time Grace yelled, "I wasn't done bidding."

"The bids have a maximum of fifteen only, Mr. Noren and Miss Kilena. Mr. Autions was the fifteenth bid, therefore, Miss Fervic goes to him."

Lander was full on grinning now. Fuck. I slumped back into my seat and refused to look back up at the stage.

By the end of the bids, Colton and Lander both had a servant. I didn't bid again. My mind kept running through every horrendous scenario of whatever the hell Lander was going to do to Lilia.

And since he was my roommate, I'd be forced to watch.

———

"Don't look so beaten up, Grey. I'll make sure to share her every now and then," Lander called as we exited the auditorium. Lilia was trailing behind us, her head down as she stared at the ground.

I ignored his comment. "Are you going to get her a healer?" I asked.

Lander smirked. "I hadn't realized you cared that much."

"I don't." I started walking toward our dorm, but I knew he was following, which meant *she* was following. "I just don't want blood on our carpet."

"She wanted to be a mender. I figured I'd do her a favor and let her mend herself."

"I don't want blood on our carpet," I repeated, because fuck me, I was going to lose my shit if she didn't get help.

He shrugged. "It's a good thing we have ourselves a little servant then. I'll have her clean it up if she does. She'll be our personal live-in maid for our suite."

I was grinding my teeth so hard my jaw hurt. Lander owned her for a total of five minutes, and he was already trying to take her to our dorm. "She's not supposed to sleep with us."

"She's mine to do whatever I want with. If you wanted a say, you should have gotten your own servant."

I didn't respond as we entered our dorm hall. Mack and Colton left to go to their own suite, leaving just Lander, Lilia, and me in ours.

She was still bleeding, and I could tell her arm was hurting her, but Lander wasn't doing anything about it.

I walked straight into the kitchen, poured myself the biggest cup of wine into the largest glass I owned, then sank down on the green sofa in our shared living room. There was no way I was going into my room now. I wasn't about to leave him alone with her, but I was going to need another five glasses of wine to be able to tolerate what the fuck was about to happen.

Honestly, I wasn't sure how far Lander would push it. I knew he was only interested in her to piss me off, but it was past the point of acting indifferent.

Lilia kept staring at the sofa. For a second, I thought she was staring at me, before I realized she'd never been in Hiwet Hall before. The living room alone was huge. It had a mini kitchenette that connected the common space to a private bath.

I was staring at the large table Lander and I never used, and for some reason, it brought me back to our childhood when I first had dinner at the Fervics. Our suite was about the size of Lilia's entire house. They didn't even have room for a table, and I had to mask my shock when they all sat on the floor to eat dinner.

"Here." Lander threw a small piece of gauze at her. "Cover your arm and then clean up your blood."

Lilia stood frozen for a moment.

"Did you hear me, Lilia?" Her eyes snapped to Lander's. He was towering over her, his stance slightly open, but the fucking possessive way he was looking at her had my mind reeling. "I guess I can call you *nix* now, since you're officially a zero."

She scowled, but it seemed to get her to move. She took a step back and started wrapping her arm one-handed. I cringed—she wasn't using any ointment. It was going to take forever to heal and stood a good chance of getting infected, which that in and of itself was super rare for an Advenian. Infections weren't common. They were considered a mortal disease, but they never cleaned the knife. They forced all of them to use the same one, and I highly doubted it was ever clean to begin with. They probably wanted them to get infected—it would further prove their stupid ideology of thinking zeroes were somehow the cause of our ancestors sleeping with mortals centuries ago.

Lilia didn't even have time to register what happened to her before she was forced into this shit. I went to take another sip from my wine but realized I already drained it.

I leaned forward to get up when Lander stopped me. "Don't." He raised his hand. "Lilia, refill Grey's wine."

I looked up at her in time to see her rip the gauze off with her teeth. She tucked the end into the wrap, but blood was already starting to stain the white material. Her eyes narrowed as she grabbed the empty glass from me.

I stared at her back as she walked into our kitchenette and slowly refilled it.

Ever since my brother's wedding, I'd envisioned bringing Lilia back here—just not like this. She paused before turning around, and my breathing hitched as her eyes flicked to mine before walking toward me.

"You know, Grey, I'd be a lot richer right now if you hadn't bid against me."

I wasn't sure what kind of response Lander wanted. Lilia shoved the glass into my hand, and I half expected her to spill it on me on purpose. But as I took it, I realized she was shaking.

I took a long sip of wine before finally answering him. "What's your point, Lander?"

"I'll share her with you if you answer something for me."

I didn't want Lilia like he thought. The idea of buying servants never sat well with me. But if it meant getting Lilia away from him, I didn't care what he thought.

"What do you want to know?" I took another sip. Lilia was standing by the door, watching us.

"Why *her*?"

I choked and started coughing as the wine went down wrong.

Lander was leaning against the counter. "You didn't bid on anyone else, so why did you bid on her?"

I shrugged. "I just wanted to see how much of your parents' money you were willing to drain."

He stopped grinning then, and I knew I fucked up. Any reminder that my family was better than his ticked him off. I shouldn't have pushed him. It was one of the long list of reasons we had a falling out and were no longer friends. If Mack and Colton picked up on the tension between us, they ignored it, but I never could.

"Come on, Lilia. We're going to hang out in my room." When she didn't move, he looked up at her, his voice lowering. "I said come here." I heard the musical hint as he used his compulsion. Lilia's feet started moving as she walked toward him. I saw the brief flicker of shock that ran through her before she tried to hide it. She was trembling.

"What the hell, Lander? Compulsion is still forbidden."

"It's forbidden on *students*, Grey. She's not a student anymore." He wrapped his hand around the small of her back, and I thought of a million different ways I could break it as he pushed her into his room and closed the door with a wink.

I couldn't fall asleep. I didn't even bother getting up to refill my wine—which I severely needed.

All I could manage was to stare at his door and wonder what the hell was happening on the other side.

SIXTEEN
LILIA

I WAS LIVING in my worst nightmare. I honestly didn't think things could get any worse. I was so scared they'd pull us out of school, but when Principal Asfon announced students were going to bid on us, I realized how foolish that thought was.

But then Alec's words hit me. *I'll put a good word in for you once you graduate. I'm in need of a servant in Palm.*

Maybe it wasn't worse. Maybe it was just the same. My future would have succumbed to this no matter where I was. But at least if I was with Alec that meant I wouldn't be forced to be around Greyland.

I had no idea why he started bidding against Lander and Grace for me. My heart accelerated as he did, and I hated that I was excited, that I felt like he actually wanted me for once. Then I remembered it was to own me, and I would have been his servant and all my anger came crashing back. No one owned me—the only person I belonged to was myself.

And if Greyland had won the bidding, my situation wouldn't be any better. He wasn't a nice Advenian.

I hated that I kept forgetting that about him. I kept confusing my reality with my fantasy.

My dreams weren't real.

But my nightmares were, and I was now living in one.

———

I DIDN'T SLEEP that night. I was too scared Lander was going to try something if I did. I spent the entire night staring at his ceiling and trying not to break down and cry while I listened to him snore.

Anytime he shifted in his bed, I swore it was going to be the moment he attacked me, but he never did.

He just slept, and I just laid there.

When he woke up, he compelled me to keep waiting on the floor. I honestly wasn't sure if I would have been able to move even if he hadn't. I was pretty sure I was going into a sleep-deprived shock.

This couldn't be real.

I was waiting for Grace to wake me up to realize that none of it actually happened.

Except it did happen. Every time I shifted on the floor, my arm would throb, and I was reminded that it wasn't a dream. It was real, and the Goddesses hated me. If they had let me go to Grace, I would have been sleeping in my own dorm room right now—

I jumped as Lander opened his bedroom door, and light poured into his room—their common area had electricity—just another reminder of the differences between the two halls.

But now things were going to get even worse...

I heard Greyland's voice coming from the other side, but Lander slammed the door shut before I could make out what he said.

Then I was alone with nothing but my thoughts. I tried to focus on my breathing, to zone out everything that had happened, because if I didn't, I knew I'd start crying.

Lander came back ten minutes later. His brown hair was damp from his bath, and he was dressed in his school uniform.

I looked down at myself. I was still wearing Grace's clothes, only the front of the blouse was covered in my blood.

"Let's go, nix."

I stood and tried not to fall as my legs felt like jello. He stared down at me before throwing his school pack in my direction. I hissed as it brushed against my cut.

Right. I wasn't taking classes anymore. I didn't need my own books, and now I'd have to follow him around all day and carry his.

I took a steadying breath, trying to dissociate from the humiliation.

I froze in their common room as soon as I saw Greyland still sitting on the green sofa.

He was staring right at me, and it felt like he could see through everything.

Lander halted in front of their door to leave their suite. "The door isn't going to open itself, *Little*."

I forced my gaze away from Greyland and tried not to focus on the fact that he was still wearing the same outfit from the night before.

———

"DID HE TOUCH YOU?"

The moment I fell asleep the next night, Dream-Greyland materialized, and he looked... pissed.

I opened my mouth, then closed it as I turned my head to the side to assess him. I'd been a servant for a total of twenty-four hours, and I only managed to drift off to sleep now.

I tried not to, but seeing Greyland in my dreams was proof that I failed, and pure exhaustion took over.

But seeing him—it almost made me happy for it, made me forget whose floor my real body was currently sleeping on. I missed this version of him. I hated that it felt like a comfort, like I finally had someone I could trust, even though none of it was real.

"Did he touch you, Lilia? Did Lander touch you?"

I shook my head, and Greyland relaxed, just a fraction.

Then his voice softened. "Are you okay?"

I was staring at my arm in my dream. I didn't know why my burn and zero came with me. I always felt like my dreams were to escape my reality…

Greyland frowned. "I want to see it—make sure it's not infected."

"This is pointless. I already looked at it myself."

"Well, *I* want to look at it now."

I scoffed but rolled my sleeve up. "This really doesn't matter."

"Humor me," Greyland said. I found myself holding my breath as he came to sit down next to me on the green sofa. "Does it hurt?"

"Yes," I admitted. This place—*my dreams*—was probably the only time I didn't have to act tough. Not that I always succeeded in reality, but at least I didn't have to try.

"It doesn't look infected, that's good, but you should put healing ointment on it."

"And where am I going to find some of that?"

"At the menders—"

I cut him off. "I'm not a student anymore, Grey."

He frowned. "So what? You aren't allowed supplies from a mender?"

"Basically." I shrugged because I already dealt with my feelings about it. I had all day to focus on it as I was forced to carry Lander's books, open doors for him, then tie and retie his boot laces purely for the fact that he liked me kneeling in front of him.

"Are they feeding you, Lilia?" I couldn't pinpoint Greyland's expression. His eyes were narrowed, and his tone was harsh, almost like it was in real life.

"Lilia," he repeated when I didn't answer.

I exhaled before rolling my sleeve back down. "We were told we can't eat during normal student hours. We have to go to the dining hall tomorrow before it opens, and they'll hand out our food for the day."

I was starving. Since I was in Lander's room all last night, I missed the announcement about food. Grace snuck cheese and dried meats into my pocket during Guard Class, but Lander took them from me the moment he saw me trying to eat them on the walk back to his room.

"On the plus side, we're still able to use the communal bathrooms in Jelckin Hall… for now," I joked. Then thought better of it and started laughing. "Not that Lander will let me set foot in Jelckin again."

"This isn't funny, Lilia."

I started belly laughing then, and I couldn't stop. Greyland just watched me, his eyes never leaving mine as I started to unravel. At some point the laughs turned to sobs.

Of course it was freaking food and a bath that had me breaking down. The dining hall and access to running water were the two things I loved most about Kitlarn Academy. We rarely ate hot meals at home, and a bath was a weekly occurrence at best—my parents couldn't afford it—so coming here, I always indulged myself in both.

Now, I wasn't even allowed to eat at the same time as my ranked classmates.

Greyland shifted on the sofa and pulled me into his lap. "I'm sorry, Lilia. I'm so fucking sorry."

I sobbed harder, watching as my tears slowly stained his shirt until eventually I fell asleep within my own dream in the comfort of Greyland Aaron Noren's arms.

———

IT HAD ONLY BEEN a week since I became Lander's servant, and I had no idea how I was going to get through the rest of the school year, let alone the rest of my life.

Miraculously, I was able to wake up on my own for the first time ever. The mornings were my only time away from Lander, and even if it only lasted twenty minutes, I wasn't going to waste it.

The first time I left his room, I nearly screamed when I saw Greyland sitting on the sofa again. He stood as soon as Lander's door closed behind me, and I froze.

I had no idea how long we both stayed like that, just staring at each other, before I came to my senses and bolted out of their suite.

Every day for the past week had been the same. I'd leave Lander's room to go get my food, and Greyland would be sitting there. He never talked to me, but I felt his eyes tracking my movements as I walked toward their door.

I tried taking the walk to the dining hall as slow as possible. Lander compelled me to get my food, then come right back to his dorm, which meant no sneaking off into Jelckin to see Grace, and after the first day when she tried to give me food, Lander made sure I wasn't able to speak with her.

I missed her. I missed the way things used to be. I could still barely wrap my head around how so much had changed in such a short time.

I was walking out of the dining hall—without tea because they only gave us what they deemed necessary to survive—when a hand pulled my shoulder.

I was about to scream before I realized it was Grace.

"Lil—" She pulled me into a hug, and everything came crashing down. All the tears I'd been shoving down came tumbling out as soon as I saw her.

"Grace," I sobbed into her shoulder.

"I'm so sorry, Lil. I tried to bid for you. I even went to Principal Asfon afterward, but he wouldn't let me—"

"It's okay, Grace." I hugged her harder, then winced as my arm pressed into her side.

She pulled back, instantly grabbing my arm and inspecting it. "Lil-ia..." she started, then stopped. Her eyes kept scanning me. "Has Lander done nothing for you since—" Her voice trailed off.

"Since I became his servant," I finished for her. I could feel his compulsion pulling me. I took a step away from Grace without wanting to. "I have to go." I tried to collect myself. The last thing I wanted to do was walk back into their dorm and let Greyland and Lander see me with swollen eyes.

Grace assessed me. "Come back to our dorm. Take a bath, and sleep in our room. Jaxs and I have been collecting extra food for you, and I have clean clothes and—"

I cut her off. That sounded like absolute heaven, and I wanted nothing more than to run back with my best friend. "Grace, I can't."

"Yes, you can, Lilia. I don't care how much money he spent on you, you should be able to sleep in your own dorm and take a bath."

"No, I mean I physically can't." I tried not to cry again. It was the first time I let myself feel anything since everything happened. The only time I cried was in my dreams, but now that I started, it was hard to hold back. "Lander's been compelling me…"

I didn't even finish before Grace started storming toward Hiwet Hall.

"Grace, wait—" I called after her, but she ignored me. She made it to Greyland and Lander's suite a second before me.

"What the hell, Lander," Grace yelled as she used her telekinesis to slam their common room door open.

Greyland was bathed and standing in the kitchen, his white shirt was unbuttoned, and his hair was dripping onto the fabric. Lander halted outside his door as he exited his room.

"Grace," he drawled before eyeing me. He didn't move from his spot and instead leaned back against the wall, putting his hands in his pocket.

"Lander Autions. Lilia needs a mender and decent food, and she shouldn't have to sleep in here with you, and she needs a bath, and new clothes, and—"

He cut her off. "Are you done, Kilena?"

Grace's hands were on her hips. "No," she huffed, a piece of her hair fell in front of her face. "I'm just getting started."

"Well, I'm done, so get out."

Grace didn't move, and I realized I was just standing behind her in the doorway like an idiot. I had no idea Grace was going to go off on him.

"I'm sorry, I'm bothering *you*," she spat. "Maybe if you didn't want to be bothered you shouldn't have bid on my best friend."

Lander pushed off the wall and started walking toward her. "I'll make sure her basic needs are met, now get the fuck out."

Grace still didn't move. "You can't use compulsion. It's banned—"

"It's banned on *students*," Lander interjected, looking down at her.

"I'll report you, Lander."

He laughed. "I'd be careful if I were you, Grace. Keep it up, and I'll report you for being a rank zero sympathizer. Somehow I think that would be worse for you than it would for me."

"Go ahead—" she started.

"Grace, stop," I cut her off. I knew she would. She'd risk repercussions to help me, but I couldn't let her.

Greyland moved out of the kitchen. "Grace is right, Lander. Lilia needs a mender and access to her dorms."

Lander turned to look at him. "Since when do you give a shit?"

Greyland's eyes narrowed. "Since our suite smells like shit because you aren't giving her basic fucking necessities like a bath, and she's been wearing the same bloody clothes for over a week."

"Fine," Lander raised his voice. He stepped around Grace and grabbed onto my arm. I cried out as his hand wrapped around my cut. He started dragging me further into their suite.

"Where the fuck are you taking her?" Greyland seethed.

"Giving her a bath like you two keep on demanding."

Greyland stepped in front of us. "In Jelkin. She needs to go back with Grace."

"We have a bath here," was all Lander said, and my pulse skyrocketed as fear overtook my senses.

Then, everything was a blur. I wasn't sure who attacked who first before Lander materialized a dagger and held it against my throat.

"Grace, get the fuck out, and Greyland back off," Lander snapped. "She is *my* slave. I won her bid, not either of you."

Greyland was fuming. "Lander," he drawled, his eyes not leaving the dagger at my throat. I was pretty sure I stopped breathing. "If you hurt her, I will fucking kill you."

"Really, Grey?" Lander laughed, and the blade dug into my neck. "Let me guess, because your brother will kill you if I touch her?"

Greyland didn't answer.

"I won't hurt her as long as you two back the fuck off." The dagger disappeared, but I barely had time to exhale before Lander pushed me into their bathroom. He turned to face Grace. "You better be gone by the time we get out, and if you use your telekinesis to open the door, I won't think twice about cutting her."

Greyland took a step toward the bathroom before Lander slammed the door shut and locked it.

He whirled on me, his body immediately flaring in golden markings. "Take off your clothes."

"You can't do this," I pleaded, but my hands had already started on the first button of my blouse.

"Then stop me, nix." He grinned and it was far from warm.

I couldn't stop him. He knew it. I knew it. And now, because of the zero burned onto my wrist, the entire kingdom knew it.

———

MERCIFULLY, Lander didn't try anything in the bath, but it was the worst ten minutes of my life.

He watched me as I undressed, then compelled me to fill the tub and stared as I was forced to bathe myself in front of him.

With the adrenaline running through me, I barely hissed as my arm met with the water. I couldn't stop trembling, could barely steady my hands long enough to even turn on the water. I was hyperventilating to the point that I swore I was going to pass out in the bath, and Lander would let me drown.

I would rather not bathe again for the rest of my life than go through this again. I wasn't sure what Lander was playing at. The anticipation of knowing he could do anything he wanted, whenever he wanted, and I could do nothing to stop him, was messing with me.

But he never did. He never touched me when we were alone. It was only when Greyland was around that he'd force me to sit on his lap or make me button his jacket or tie his shoes. On the days Greyland wasn't in their suite, he didn't bother with bringing me into their bathroom to bathe. But when he was there, this became our new routine.

He even started forcing me to hand feed him in the dining hall until Greyland stopped coming.

I was terrified for the day his boredom or curiosity would take over, and regardless of whether Greyland was around to see it, it wouldn't be a game to him anymore.

SEVENTEEN
GREYLAND

THE PAST COUPLE of weeks were pure hell. Lander kept Lilia in our dorm whenever we weren't in classes, and I knew he only did it to flaunt her in front of me. He was trying to get a rise out of me, and it was working. I hadn't slept in my own bed since the Bidding. Most nights I opted to lay on the sofa and nurse way too much wine as I tried to listen through his door.

Watching her with him was slowly killing me, and the more I saw, the harder it was for me to deny my feelings toward her.

At first I convinced myself it was just because I knew her family. But I couldn't shake the jealousy. Couldn't rid myself of the pure anger I felt whenever Lander touched her.

I stayed on the guard mats an extra two hours after classes ended today, trying to blow off some steam. Not that it fixed any of my problems. All I could think about was pale blonde hair and hazel eyes.

I couldn't avoid it anymore, couldn't avoid *her*. I had to go back to my suite.

"Ah, Grey, you just missed it," Lander slurred as I walked into our dorm and right into a fucking party.

One glance at Mack and Colton told me they were drunk from trying to keep up with Lander. The guy could out drink all of us.

Colton's servant was sitting on his lap, and a few other classmates were well into their own drinks—some with servants, some without. I didn't know half their names, and the ones I did know, I didn't care about. Our common room was spacious, but Lander invited enough people to fill it.

I kept scanning the room until I found hazel eyes. Lilia was standing against the wall. Her hands were pressed together, and I knew she was trying to hide the tremble in them.

"Missed what?" I asked.

"I just compelled Lilia to reveal her sex life."

Everyone laughed, but Lander didn't take his eyes off me. He was lounging on the sofa, his legs spread with an empty glass of wine resting in his hand.

I held my breath. I wasn't sure if I wanted to know. I didn't say anything, just stood in the door, trying to rein in my temper. Mack and Colton's laughs started to fade as they realized my unease.

Lander stood, tossing his empty glass of wine on the floor. A male servant—I only knew from the zero branded into him—started picking up the shattered glass and cleaning the floor.

"Complete virgin." Lander grinned as he walked toward her, and Lilia froze. "She's never even been properly kissed."

"I think the whole school knew she was prude," I said, trying to remain calm, but his hand was against her neck, and I wanted nothing more than to rip it off her.

Lander grinned. "You're right. But we did find something out that no one knows."

A tear ran down Lilia's face as a few more people laughed. She was still pressed against the wall, still ramrod straight like she couldn't move. Lander's body flared in golden markings. "Tell Grey what you told us about being kissed."

I wasn't breathing. Lilia was shaking now, her eyes purposely avoiding mine. "I…" she started, then stopped, trying to fight the compulsion.

"Today, Lilia." Lander rolled his eyes.

"I've only ever been kissed in my dreams." More tears escaped down her cheeks. Her voice was quiet, but I heard every fucking syllable.

"And who do you have sex dreams about?" Lander was still compelling her.

Her hazel eyes whipped to his, widening a fraction.

"Stop this," I said. "If this is your idea of fun, you're more pathetic than I thought." I pushed past them into the kitchen and opened a new bottle of wine. "Who the hell cares who she dreams about?"

"Oh, I'm just getting started, Grey. You see, I was telling Colt and Mack what a shame it was that Little's never been touched. She has such a nice rack, it shouldn't go to waste. But it's funny, they had no idea what I was talking about."

Well, fuck.

"Any ideas on how that could happen?" he asked me.

"I have no idea what you're talking about." I turned to face him, completely forgetting about the wine I just opened. He moved Lilia in front of him, forcing her to face me.

Lander kept grinning. "I thought I'd rectify that."

Before I could blink, he materialized a dagger in his free hand and ran it up her school uniform. By the time I moved, her shirt was in shreds by her feet. The servant who was cleaning the floor swore as he jumped out of the way.

"This is ending, right now." I pushed Lander away from her, ripping the dagger out of his hand. It disappeared as soon as I threw it across the room. Not that it mattered, he had another one already materialized. He swiped at me, forcing me to take a step back, a step away from her.

"Calm down, Grey. I'm just having a little fun." It was all he needed. He had her pants cut off in the next breath.

I ignored him and stormed over to her. There was no way I was standing by and letting this happen. I had been holding myself back for weeks now, but I couldn't take it anymore.

"What the hell, Grey? You don't own her. I do," Lander spat. "And I can do whatever the hell I want with *my* property."

"No one owns her," I seethed as I started to push her toward my room.

"I'm pretty sure that's the definition of a servant." Lander took a step toward us. "I bought her so she's mine."

"No. She's meant to help hold your books or some other bullshit, not be fucking made to stand there while you cut her clothes off or forced to sleep in your room every night."

Colton's servant was ramrod straight on his lap, but at least she still had clothes on.

"I didn't realize you liked her."

I stilled, my back to Lander. My hand was gripping Lilias's bare arm, and I hated the fact that she was still trembling. "I don't."

"To me it looks like you're jealous."

"I'm not." I relaxed my hand, not realizing my grip had tightened around her arm.

"Could have fooled me," Lander challenged.

"I just don't feel like getting a black eye because of you," I lied, knowing everyone was watching us. I looked over my shoulder to meet his gaze. "She's my brother's best friend's little sister. If he finds out what you're doing to her, Sie will beat the living shit out of me."

"Sure, if that's what you want to tell yourself, Grey," Lander called.

I started dragging Lilia toward my room again but stopped and turned to Mack. "If you use your telekinesis to unlock my door, you're dead, and I can promise you that my wrath will be a lot worse than Lander's." Then I pushed Lilia into my room and turned the lock.

She halted by the door. As soon as I dropped my grip on her arm, her own hands clutched her abdomen. I stormed toward my dresser and threw a long black t-shirt at her. I heard her shrug it on. "I can give you pants, but they'll be too big. You'll swim in them."

When she didn't answer, I turned to her. "Lilia, do you want pants?"

She nodded. I found the smallest pair I owned and met her across the room. "Here."

"Th-thanks." She took them from my hands, making sure to avoid any skin contact, then bent forward to put them on.

Yup, they were huge on her, but some part of me loved it—loved seeing her in my clothes. *Probably cause you're fucked up, Greyland. She just had one of the worst nights of her life, and you're fantasizing about her wearing your clothes.*

"You can take my bed."

Her head snapped up. "What?"

"Unless you want to go back to Lander."

Her eyes narrowed. "And I'm supposed to believe you're any better?"

"Well, I'm not going to compel you." She wasn't backing down. I sighed, running my hand over my face. "Yes, Lilia. I'm better than Lander. I won't hurt you. Just sleep on the bed. I'll take the floor."

"Greyland?"

"Lilia."

"I um… drank a lot. Lander forced me to…" She paused, biting her lip, and I waited a good minute for her to continue, but she didn't. She just kept staring at the hem of my sweatpants bundled around her feet.

"Lilia, I'm not going to take advantage of you because you're drunk—"

"No, it's not that. But um… I have to pee."

"You're shitting me, right? The bathroom is back in the common room."

She bit her lip again. "I know, but I really, *really* have to pee."

I grunted. "Fine. I'll cast my illusion on us to make it look like we didn't leave the room, but I'm coming with you, and you can't make a sound."

"Okay." She started hiccuping, and I realized just how drunk she was. Fuck Lander.

"I mean it, Lilia, you can't make a sound."

"I won't. I'll hold my breath," she promised.

I eyed her for another minute before calling my powers. I focused on our living room, on the bodies still drinking and partying and started altering the room. First, I put my illusion on my door, making it appear closed even after I opened it. Then I put it into the path we'd take and didn't stop until it wrapped around the bathroom.

I turned, gesturing for Lilia to come.

She gathered my pants, pulling them up at the hem so she wouldn't trip. Thankfully, she didn't hiccup during the walk. It wasn't until I closed the bathroom door that she let out a sound.

"Hurry up," I said, turning my back to her to give her privacy.

I heard her shuffle then curse as she hit something. A hiccup followed a second later. I waited for what felt like five minutes and heard nothing coming from her. "Lilia?"

Another hiccup. "What?"

"Why aren't you peeing?"

"I can't with you listening."

I rolled my eyes, then turned the faucet on. She squealed as it put her in my periphery. I caught a quick glance of her legs before I turned back around. "Hurry up, Lil, before someone else has to pee and realizes we're in here."

I heard her huff, and then a second later a stream sounded. She wasn't joking, she had to pee a lot.

"Shit," I cursed as the door handle jiggled from the other side. I didn't bother waiting to see if Lilia was decent before I bolted toward her—thankfully, she was.

I came up behind her, putting my hand over her mouth as I pressed her back against my chest. "Don't make a sound," I whispered into her ear. I felt her head move in a nod beneath my grip and that was good enough for me.

"What the fuck is wrong with your door, Land?" someone drawled as they tried the knob again. I quickly unlatched the lock before pressing Lilia and I against the wall, casting my illusion over us until only a blank wall was visible.

I watched the door open and Penson, one of Lander's friends I fucking hated, walked in. He locked the door and started making his way toward the toilet. I created another illusion into the bowl, getting rid of the toilet paper Lilia had used. She stiffened under me like she just now realized she was going to see him unbutton his pants before he started pissing.

My hand was still over her mouth, and I suddenly became hyper aware of how soft her lips felt.

Penson burped before walking over to the mirror and started fixing his hair.

"Capri," he called, still staring at his own reflection, and I stiffened. He wasn't leaving. A moment later, a girl with red hair and brown eyes stepped into the door frame.

"Yes?" she asked.

Shit. Shit. Shit.

"I need your help," Penson slurred, and I realized just how drunk he was. How drunk they all were.

The girl frowned. She had a matching zero on her wrist just like Lilia's. "With what?"

Penson gestured to the button on his pants.

"Get lost, Penson. I'm not doing that."

"You're my servant. You have to do what I tell you."

Lilia's lips parted beneath my grip. I could feel her breath against my palm as her breathing quickened.

"You and your friends can go to hell. You think just because you spent money that I owe you anything?"

Penson smiled. "It's not like you haven't done it before."

"Yeah, and it was a mistake. I'm not doing this."

His demeanor shifted. Capri squealed as he pulled her the rest of the way into the bathroom and pinned her against the sink.

"Lander," Penson raised his voice. "I need you for a second."

Shit. I had to get Lilia out of here *now*, but they were too close to the door.

A second later Lander came in. "What?"

"Compel her for me, will you?" Penson asked.

"Seriously?" I could tell he was pissed off. If it was anyone else that had grabbed Lilia, they'd be on the floor by now, but Lander knew I could beat him, and he didn't want to risk losing in front of a crowd.

"Yeah, just cause you're in a piss-poor mood doesn't mean we all have to be," Penson slurred. I glanced at Capri. She was half shaking, half fuming.

Lander looked between them. "Fine, but then I want to borrow her when you're done." There was no way Lilia was going to watch this.

She tensed beneath me as we listened to Lander's compulsion, and I had to tighten my grip around her mouth because I was terrified she was going to speak up and blow our cover.

As soon as Lander left, Penson dragged Capri further into the bathroom. I shifted my illusion from the wall to the door and slowly opened it so only Lilia and I could see.

As soon as we were back in my room with the door locked, I exhaled. I didn't care how badly Lilia had to pee, we weren't leaving again.

She whirled on me as I let go of her arm. "You have to stop it."

"Stop what?"

"Capri. What they're trying to do. You need to do something."

"Just because I pulled you away, doesn't mean I can do that for everyone."

She frowned. "It's not right, Grey. You can't let—"

"Lilia," I cut her off. "What's happening right now is fucked up, but it's nothing new. This is how servants are treated. In my home, in many others around Tennebris. I can't stop this. It's beyond you and me."

Tears were welling in her eyes.

"Maybe when your brother—"

I cut her off again, and she flinched. "Go to sleep, Lilia."

I didn't want to talk about Sie. I knew my brother would try to change things. He wouldn't let things get this fucked, but I couldn't promise Lilia anything, not when I didn't even know if Sie would be alive long enough to try.

Everything was going to shit, and I was terrified this was only the beginning.

EIGHTEEN
LILIA

"I HATE YOU." By the time I finally drifted off to sleep, the alcohol was starting to wear off.

"I know," Dream-Greyland said softly. I was sitting on the sofa with my knees pulled to my chest, hugging my legs.

Grey materialized as he always did, but he didn't make his way toward the sofa. He looked stunned, wary even. He just stood there watching me...

He kept looking like he knew exactly what happened tonight—I guess he did since he was a figment of my imagination—but I wanted to forget it. I *needed* to forget it. All of it. I had no idea how I managed to fall asleep, but I was already crying in my dreams.

I hated it. I hated the look he was still giving me. It made me relive it all, made it impossible to forget what just happened. Made me think of Capri and what she had to do in the bathroom, and the realization dawned on me that if he hadn't pulled me into his room tonight, the same thing could have happened to me...

"No, you don't know. I hate you so much, Greyland, you have no idea."

"I hate myself too, Lilia." He was still standing in front of the sofa. "I'm sorry."

I half laughed, half sobbed. "For what, Grey?"

"All of it."

I wasn't sure how long I cried before my tears finally dried. I wiped my eyes and looked up, realizing that Greyland still hadn't moved. He was just standing there, staring at me.

"You can sit down, you know."

He still didn't move.

"You just need to hang on a little bit longer, Lilia," he said, before turning his head toward that endless gray space. Banging sounded before I was pulled from my dream.

My eyes blinked as I adjusted to the light in Greyland's room.

The banging got louder, and I realized that someone was pounding on Greyland's door. One glance across his room and I saw he had been sleeping on the floor.

He stood, glaring at the door, and I realized he was wearing the same outfit he had on in my dreams. I didn't even remember seeing him change before sleep found me.

My head was pounding from all the alcohol Lander made me drink.

"Stay there," Greyland shot at me before he strode over to the door and only then did I realize I was still in his bed.

I slept in Greyland Aaron Noren's bed last night.

He slept on the floor—but still. All those nights of dreaming what his room would be like, and here I was in it.

Greyland swung his door open with a resounding thud. "What do you want?"

Lander was on the other side, a fist in the air, about to bang on the wood again. "I want my servant back," he sneered.

"No."

Lander was staring at me over Greyland's shoulder before his one-worded answer made him snap his attention back to Grey.

"What did you just say?" he spat.

"I said no," Greyland repeated, then added, "Lilia, we're leaving."

"What?" I wasn't sure if I heard him right. I technically belonged to Lander. Could Grey really just keep me? I hated that a small part of me was excited about it—or relieved—I couldn't tell. Because I did not want to spend another minute alone with Lander Autions.

I was terrified he was going to force himself on me now that he knew I was a virgin. The more time I spent around him, the more he pushed his limits. He made comments about it, compelled me to answer truths I never wanted to admit.

At first I swore he was only using me to piss Greyland off. Before all this happened, I thought they were friends, but now, I was second guessing everything. They seemed to *hate* each other. Whenever Lander did anything, Grey looked five seconds away from murdering him.

But as the weeks dragged on, I found Lander staring more even when Greyland wasn't around.

"I'm taking you home for the weekend," Greyland said as he turned to look at me. I was still sitting on his bed, still wearing his clothes. My cheeks reddened as I thought back to how close I was to admitting to Grey that I dreamed about him. I hated that Lander now knew it, that he almost compelled me to tell him. I hated it even more that despite everything that happened, I still couldn't stop.

"What the fuck, Grey. She's my slave," Lander sneered.

"She's a *servant*, not a fucking *slave*, Lander."

"Same thing and that doesn't mean you can keep taking her. She's mine."

Greyland shrugged. "I don't have a choice. My mother arranged it and told me I had to bring her. She'll be back before classes start on Monday."

"Fine, but what you did last night," his voice lowered as his gaze flicked over to me, "you can't pull that again. I let it slide, but I won't next time."

Greyland ignored him.

I felt Lander's eyes on me again before he changed the subject. "Are they really letting a zero attend your brother's coronation just because her brother is going to be the second?"

"I have no idea, Lander. I was just told to bring her." Greyland turned to look at me again. "Hurry up. We're leaving in ten minutes."

"I... I don't have my things."

Greyland's eyes narrowed. "Go pack then. I'll meet you at your dorm."

I didn't need to be told twice. I had no idea if I was really going to attend Sie's coronation, but I didn't care as long as it got me away from Lander.

I ran out of Grey's room without looking back.

NINETEEN
GREYLAND

"So THIS IS the big weekend for Sie, huh?" Lander asked as soon as Lilia ran out. He followed me into my room, watching me throw things into a bag of my own.

I knew he was pissed at me, but I also knew he wouldn't try to get me back, not yet at least. He made it clear. My name and influence would only work for so long.

"Yup," I said, trying to ignore him as I continued to pack.

"What's tonight again?"

"Some pre-celebration thing with Lux."

"Tomorrow's the actual coronation, then?" he asked.

I nodded, not bothering to look at him.

"Do I have to call you prince when you get back?"

"I don't fucking care what you call me." I zipped up my bag and flung it over my shoulder. "I'm going to be late."

———

I THREW healing ointment and an apple on her lap as soon as Lilia got into my car.

Her eyes widened. "What is—"

"It's for your arm."

She picked up the ointment and immediately took a bite out of the apple. I figured they were barely feeding her. I hadn't seen a zero eating in the dining hall since they became servants, and over the past three weeks, it looked like she'd lost weight.

"Thank you."

I nodded and started driving toward Kitlarn immediately. We were quiet for the first fifteen minutes of the ride. Lilia was staring out the window, refusing to look at me. I didn't blame her. I hated that she didn't put the ointment on her arm, but I figured she wouldn't do it in front of me.

"I'm not really going to the coronation, am I?" she asked after a while.

"No."

"Why am I here, Grey?"

"My mother—"

"Spare me the fake cover. Why am I *really* here?"

I looked at her for a split second before I had to focus back on the road. I wasn't going to admit that I was fucking terrified for my brother's coronation. I didn't want to scare her. Sie told me he thought Synder was trying to kill him just like he had Lunder, and if something was going to happen, it would be this weekend. I thought back to the cabin Sie teleported me to. I needed Lilia where I could get to her quickly. She was safer with her parents than at the school.

"I figured you could use a break from Lander. He's a dick," I settled on, which was still the truth.

"He's your friend," she said it like a question, but she knew the answer. Ever since he bid on Lilia, I couldn't pretend to like him anymore.

"No, he's not."

"Could have fooled me." She turned to look at me. She was silent for a minute before she added, "You know you're a dick too."

"Well aware, Lilia."

She was quiet again, but I could still feel her looking at me. "Just spit it out. What do you want to ask?"

"I—" she started, then stopped. "How did you know I wanted to ask something?"

"Because you bite your bottom lip when you're holding back a question."

I was glad I was driving right now because it gave me a distraction. I didn't want to see her face after I just admitted to watching her. But I couldn't help it anymore. Every second I got, I found myself staring at her lips.

"I was wondering if you ever asked your mom about my brother. I still haven't heard from him."

"Lilia, I'm sorry."

Her silky hair grazed my arm as she whipped her head to me. "What happened? Is he okay?"

"Yeah, he's fine—"

She sank back into her seat, her posture relaxing. "Oh. You said sorry, so I thought…" Her voice trailed off.

"Shit. No. Why would you assume that?"

"Because I've never heard you apologize in your entire life. I assumed if you were now it meant—"

"I'm not a complete asshole," I bit out. She didn't respond, which I guess I deserved. "I saw Sie when I went home a few weekends back. Your brother's fine, but he's in Lux."

"What? Why?"

"Scotlind Rumor isn't a zero. She's Luxian. The whole thing was a set up."

She gasped, and I took my eyes off the road long enough to see her lips parted.

I knew I probably shouldn't have told her. Not that I thought she'd do anything with the information, but Lander could easily compel it out of her. It just felt wrong not to. She deserved to know and it wasn't like Peter wasn't going to fill her in the next time they saw each other. I knew the two of them were super close.

"After the first broadcast, they shipped her off to Lux. Your brother went looking for her. Sie told me he'd be back tonight, so I'll see him at the castle." I stole a glance at her and found her looking out the window again. "You don't seem surprised."

"I assumed they were using Scotlind as an excuse to do this to us," she admitted softly. "I just thought she was a zero, but I guess it makes sense if she's Luxian since they can be compelled too."

"Yeah."

Neither of us spoke the rest of the drive.

By the time I pulled into her parent's drive, I was on edge. I couldn't stop this gut wrenching feeling that things were going to get worse. I was terrified for my brother, scared shitless that Synder was going to try something this weekend. But then I was more anxious to get this weekend over with. I needed Sie to become king, and then I needed to ask him the biggest fucking favor of my life because there was no way I was bringing Lilia back to Lander.

I knew my brother would try. If not for me, for Peter. But I also knew I was fucking delusional.

I watched Lilia get out of the car. She changed out of my clothes, and I found myself disappointed. I assumed she was wearing another outfit of Grace's because it was way too small on her.

"Lilia," I started, and she paused. Her hazel eyes met mine. "Don't leave your house this weekend. Don't go into town."

"Why?"

"Just trust me." I drove off before she could say anything else.

TWENTY
LILIA

"Lilia, what are you doing here?" my mother's voice reached me as soon as I walked through the front door. A second later, I was engulfed in a hug.

"Greyland drove me home," I managed to get out in between her squeezing.

"Your father and I were so worried. We were trying to save enough money to come visit the school. Once we heard what happened—"

"I'm fine, Mum." I shrugged out of her grip and was finally able to see her face. It was so much like mine. Eyes that weren't brown or green but somewhere in between. Small dimples that were easy to miss. We even had the same silky hair that wouldn't hold a curl. But her face looked withered—stressed. Tears immediately swelled in her eyes and rolled down her cheeks.

"Thank the Goddess," my father's voice came from behind us. "I thought I heard you." His hand was clutching his heart as he halted in the door frame separating the kitchen from the front entrance—which also doubled as the opening into our living space. The kitchen was only big enough for two people to stand in at a time and the walkway was too narrow for both of us to pass through.

"Hi, Dad." I gave a smile as I sidestepped my mother. He was instantly at my side, pulling me into a hug. He looked more like Peter, except his eyes were fully brown while my brother's were bright green.

"Have a seat." Mum gestured toward the living room. "I'll get some food for us."

Three minutes later we were sitting on the floor with dried meat in front of us. My parents let me eat more than my share, and I was thankful. I was starving. The meals we were given at school were barely enough to last the day.

"What happened? Are they treating you okay?" Mum asked, her eyes kept scanning my left arm—where my cut and rank zero brand were hidden beneath my sleeve. I kept Grace's coat on, not wanting either of them to see the brand. The ointment Greyland had given me was still in my pocket untouched. I had no idea what to make of it. He was the last person I expected to help me.

"Everything is fine, Mum." I willed myself not to think about the past couple of weeks, and especially not about last night. I couldn't explain what was happening to my parents. I couldn't get the words out to tell them they basically sold us to our classmates and none of the teachers were stepping in to stop it, even as they openly saw the mistreatment.

"We heard they took you out of classes, that they had some bidding—"

"Mum, we're still in school. We're just taking servant classes instead," I lied. The meat in my stomach was starting to stir. "Have you heard from Peter?" I asked.

She started crying more, and Dad frowned. I felt slightly guilty for changing the subject. My parents adored Peter, and if anything was going to steer the conversation away from me, it would be my brother.

I knew they probably hadn't, that it was wrong of me to bring him up, but if he was going to be at Sie's coronation tomorrow morning, there was a chance he had stopped here first.

"We haven't," Dad said. "We figured he's busy at the castle with everything that's been happening. I'm sure he'll visit us soon."

I nodded. I wasn't about to explain to them what Greyland had told me. For one, my parents would freak out, and two, I was fairly certain it was confidential. I doubted Greyland was even allowed to tell me, and my traitorous mind kept repeating—*why did he tell you?*

Then I would spiral and replay everything from last night...

Greyland had dropped me off early in the morning, and my parents and I talked all day. It was mostly me diverting all the questions they asked about school, but it was nice seeing them. By the time they went on their nightly walk together, I was exhausted. I made my way toward my shared room with Peter, planning on falling asleep early.

I'd barely been sleeping. Most nights it was only pure exhaustion that had me dozing off on Lander's floor. I was excited to go into my dreamland, not only to finally sleep without Lander nearby but because I wanted to see *him*.

I realized that Dream-Greyland was the only person I could be completely open with, which was pathetic. I didn't even tell Grace or my brother everything that I told Dream-Grey.

I opened the door to my childhood room and everything hit me at once. I could barely hold back my tears as I opted to sleep on my brother's cot instead of mine.

I missed Peter so much.

Half of me wished I was invited to the coronation with the real Greyland. Not that I had any desire to be around the High Council or Synder or any of the males trying to make my life worse. But I needed to see my brother. It was the longest we'd ever been apart.

I just barely pulled his blanket over me when the door burst open.

Greyland was standing in the door frame. His dark gaze was wide and he was... panting.

I rubbed my eyes. I hadn't fallen asleep yet, had I?

Because there was no way Greyland Noren was standing inside my bedroom if it wasn't a dream...

TWENTY-ONE
GREYLAND

I ran over to her. She winced as I grabbed her wrist, before pulling her out of bed. "Shit, sorry," I swore, completely forgetting about her brand.

"Grey," her voice was groggy like she was just about to fall asleep. I saw her rub her eye with her free hand as I moved her through her house. It'd been years since I last was in their home, and I'd forgotten how damn small it was.

She tripped as we made it to the front of her house. I caught her under the ribs, steadying her before I tore through her home.

"Shit," I cursed again.

I went through every room three times, but no one else was here. Why the fuck did this all have to happen when no one was home? I tried not to think about the fact that I couldn't find my own mother. I checked for her car at the castle before I left, but it wasn't there.

"Lilia, where are your parents?" I asked her as I sprinted back to where I left her. Her hazel eyes were wide. Distantly, I heard her asking me over and over again what was happening, but I ignored it.

"They're on their walk," she started, "they walk together every night—"

I didn't wait for her to finish before I was pulling her out the door. I heard everything I needed to know. They weren't home, and we didn't have time to wait for them.

I needed to come back for my mother. If she wasn't at the castle, she had to be here in Kitlarn. I'd look for Lilia's parents then.

But the guilt was eating away at me—I came for Lilia before I went to my own home.

She was okay, my mother was okay…

"Grey, what's happening?" she asked again, this time pulling back against my grip.

I swore before turning to face her, not loosening my hold on her wrist. "We don't have time right now. We need to run. I'll explain later." I started pulling her again, dragging her to the perimeter of her home where it met with the woods.

"Run, Lilia," I said again because fuck, if we had any hope of surviving, she needed to be faster.

TWENTY-TWO
LILIA

GREYLAND NEVER LET GO of my wrist as he dragged me through the woods between Kitlarn and Palm. I wanted to ask him so many questions, but I bit them back.

Why was he in Kitlarn instead of Palm?

Why did he come to my home?

Why did he ask where my parents were?

Why were we running?

The list went on and on. But I could barely focus, could hardly think beyond sprinting and trying to keep up with him.

I swore so many times he was going to pull my arm out of its socket, but he didn't stop. It only made me more paranoid. Adrenaline was pumping through me, and my heart was beating so erratically it was all I could hear.

Greyland Noren was one of the most collected Advenians I'd ever met. I'd seen him an angry calm countless times before but never like this. To see him this panicked—

I had no idea how long we were running before he finally slowed. We weren't on a normal path. Nothing was paved. There was no indication of life. All there was were thick trees and broken branches that I had to focus on not tripping over.

"Greyland," I wheezed, my lungs were burning, and my legs were shaking, all I wanted to do was collapse. I wasn't used to this, didn't train in the guard like he had.

He turned to look at me. His eyes roaming my body before settling on mine. He still hadn't let go of my wrist, and he was abnormally pale, even for him. Whatever was happening—it terrified him.

"What's going on?" I huffed between breaths.

"My brother..." his voice was just as breathless as mine. "They imprisoned him."

I stopped, shock coursing through me, but he tugged at my arm. "Keep walking, Lilia."

"Wh-what happened?"

"I don't know. By the time I got there, things were already going to shit."

"Is my brother—"

"I don't know, Lilia," he cut me off. "I didn't even get inside the castle. I only made it to the parking deck before I heard what happened. I drove back to Kitlarn right away."

"Why?"

"We need to go into hiding," was all he said.

I was thankful we weren't sprinting anymore. He had picked up the pace to more of a brisk walk, and it was enough to get me to stop talking.

My legs were cramping, and my body had never been pushed this hard before. The dried meat I had with my parents wasn't enough to hold me over and my vision was starting to blur as dizziness took over.

Every part of me was sweating from exertion, but my feet—they were frozen, so numb that I couldn't feel my toes. We left in such a rush I didn't have time to grab shoes. Then it dawned on me. I just finished dinner with my parents. They were on their walk just like they did every night. "Grey, my parents. They're still in Kitlarn—"

"I know."

"We have to go back and get them." I tried tugging his arm in the opposite direction, but it was no use. He kept walking, half dragging me with him.

"I'll get them, Lilia. I have to go back for my mother too."

"Let's get them now. We can—"

He cut me off. "I have to get you safe first."

"Why?"

"Why what?" he snapped, but he didn't look at me. He kept walking, kept turning his head to scan our surroundings.

"Why do you have to get *me* safe first?" I couldn't stop the question rolling off my tongue. My mind kept repeating the simple phrase, even though it was the least pressing thing he'd said.

I felt his fingers tighten around my wrist. My own pulse was pounding erratically, and I wasn't sure if it was from running anymore. We'd been walking for hours.

"I made a promise to my brother."

"You promised Sie…" My voice trailed off as I switched my question mid-thought. "Wait. He knew this would happen?" I asked, then something else dawned on me. "Did *you* know this was going to happen?"

He shook his head, his dark hair was plastered across his forehead despite the cold air. "Not entirely. My brother guessed something like this might happen. He thought Synder was trying to overthrow him, but he wasn't sure."

There was a rotting cabin ahead of us.

He guided me toward the door, and neither of us said anything as he opened it, and we walked inside. There was a fireplace with cut wood next to it. Multiple bedrolls along the wall and a small table with tucked in chairs positioned in the middle of the room. Buckets of water and canned food were across from me.

"Lilia," Grey said, his voice lowering as he turned to face me. "I need you to promise me something."

"What is this place?" I asked, ignoring his question. I couldn't stop looking around, taking it all in.

"It's an old cabin our brothers used to come to." He grabbed my face in his hands, and I stilled. His dark eyes found mine and there was fear in them. Fear and something else I couldn't comprehend.

"Lilia, I need you to promise me that you'll stay here. Stay here, and don't leave this cabin no matter what."

"But my parents, my brother—" If something happened to Sie. If Greyland was this concerned that he brought me here... he said we had to go into hiding. He must have thought they were going to come after both of our families...

"I'll get them, Lilia. I'll get them all, but you need to stay here. You're not safe in Kitlarn."

I didn't answer. I didn't know how. The only sound I made was my ragged breathing.

"Lilia. I'll get them," he said again. "I promise you I'll come back, but now I need you to promise me..."

"Okay," I whispered softly, not recognizing my own voice. He was standing so close to me, his breathing hovering over my mouth. "I promise."

He still hadn't let go of my face. I wasn't entirely sure I wanted him to. His gaze softened, like my promise was the answer he needed.

He stared at me for three long seconds, then he took a step closer.

I closed my eyes, hoping, wishing for more, but then my cheeks were cold as he let me go.

The door to the cabin was left swinging, and Greyland was already sprinting back toward Kitlarn before I could think better of it.

TWENTY-THREE
GREYLAND

I FIGURED it had to be close to morning by the time I sprinted back to Kitlarn.

I went to Lilia's house first. It was closer to the perimeter of the woods, but as I approached, I knew I was too late.

I forgot I drove here, that I left my car in front of their home. The engine had still been running when I sprinted inside to get her, and now it was damaged beyond repair. It was ransacked—the windshield was shattered, the steering wheel ripped off, and the tires were all slashed.

I scanned the outside of their home. Their front door was kicked in, pieces of wood were missing by the handle, but the most alarming part was that it was left open. No one in their right mind left their doors open in Tennebris—it was too cold—and I knew the Fervics didn't have enough money for a fireplace.

I waited in the tree cover, listening to hear if anyone was still inside. Then I called to my ability, casting an illusion from the woods to their home, taking my time tracking the path I'd take to get there. It wasn't as effective. If I couldn't physically see the person I was casting an illusion on, it was a gamble if it'd even work.

No one jumped me as I started walking across their lawn, so either my illusion was working or I was alone.

I stilled in the door frame, my breath leaving my lungs in a span of a second.

There was blood everywhere. I spotted Lilia's dad first. There were pieces of him scattered across their living room, probably from the work of an energy weaponry user.

I took slow even breaths and forced myself to step into the threshold. If there was a chance her mother was still alive, I owed it to her to find out—

I didn't have to look long before I found pale blonde hair in the kitchen. Lilia's mother was prone, but her head was angled just enough for me to see. I wish I hadn't. Her lips were still parted like she'd been screaming. She was cut from the waist up. I noticed her hand was missing before I forced myself to look away.

The uncanny resemblance she had to Lilia had my heart racing. I had to remind myself it wasn't her. I got her out. Lilia was safe in the cabin. She was whole.

Guilt washed through me. Were they dead because of me? Because I left evidence that I was here? It was stupid. I should have thought everything through before I drove to their house…

My thoughts stilled as realization dawned on me. If they had my brother imprisoned, they weren't stopping until they had all the Norens. Which meant my mother—

I started sprinting toward the outskirts of town where our house was. I wasn't paying attention to the amount of people that most likely spotted me, or the fact that I was dragging the Fervic's blood through the streets. All I could think about was my own mother getting cut into pieces. I knew they'd draw it out. The Council would take their time with her death if she was caught.

The gate was still intact by the time I neared my home.

I sprinted toward the back. I wasn't about to risk opening it. I climbed the only part of the fence that wasn't monitored and quietly jumped down onto my property before I heard a raspy voice.

"It was foolish of you to come back home, Greyland."

I looked up in time to see Synder step into view. There was a crown on his head, obscuring his greasy hair and reminding me that my brother wasn't the king.

Only then did I realize my body wasn't covered in golden markings. I had dropped my illusion without realizing it. I scanned our backyard, but my mother was nowhere to be found.

———

"LILIA."

Thank Pylemo, she finally fell asleep. I'd been so worried that she wouldn't and my powers would be taken from me before she went to bed.

"Grey?" Her voice drifted to me as she came into view. It was always the same. Just her with a graying world around us until I materialized more. I usually brought in a green sofa, a blanket, anything I thought we might need… I didn't bother with it now.

I could tell she only just fell asleep. Her words were groggy as she tried to focus, but I pulled her in too fast, forcing her into our dreamscape.

"Hi—" she started, but I cut her off. We didn't have time to pretend anymore.

"Lilia, listen to me. You can't leave. You need to stay in the cabin."

Her hazel eyes widened as she took in my frantic state. I didn't have time to shift what I was wearing. How she was seeing me was how I looked in the real world. I was covered in blood. My shirt was ripped and—

I realized a second too late I still had shackles clamped around my wrists. Her eyes shifted to them, and she stumbled, taking a step back, but there was nothing for her to trip on, nowhere for her to go except my endless mind I brought her into.

"What's happening?"

I took a step toward her, closing the distance and grabbed her hands. My chains rattled before I thought better of it and made them disappear.

"I have two abilities—" I started.

"No." She took a step back. Her hazel eyes widening as she frantically shook her head. "No."

"Lilia, listen to me. This is real. We're talking. It's not your subconscious, and I need you to hear everything I have to say."

"No," she said again, and I knew she was going into shock. I took her face in my hands.

"You need to stay in the cabin. Don't come looking for me." I took a deep breath, preparing myself for what I had to say next. "And I'm sorry. I couldn't save them."

I watched in horror as her mind worked. I hated doing it, hated being the one to tell her that I was too late, and her parents were already dead by the time I ran back to her house. But she needed to know. She had to understand there was no one to come back to. That nothing of importance was worth leaving for now.

She had to know because if she left… if they caught her too…

"No…" her voice drifted, and I knew she was making the connections. "No. This isn't real. This is just my subconscious—"

"Lilia," I interrupted because I didn't have time. My real body was being transferred to Palm. It was only a matter of time before they put Alluse shackles on me, and I would lose access to my powers. "This isn't your mind. It's my ability. I have dream manipulation. It's me. I'm really here."

I watched as realization dawned on her. All those dreams she had since ninth year had been because of me. It wasn't her mind. It was all me, all because I couldn't stay away.

At first I did it by accident. I went to bed one night thinking about her, but once I realized how she reacted to me, how she treated me differently thinking it wasn't real, I became addicted. I knew it was wrong. She thought it was her own brain conjuring me up.

It was the only reason she was so open and honest, and I craved it, craved her, craved the rawness she gave me.

I was a fucking asshole.

"I—I don't understand."

"Every night, I've been here." I let my embarrassment go. I was never going to see her again, so it didn't matter anyway. All that mattered now was that she stayed alive and in that cabin. "It was me forcing you into my mind when you fell asleep," I said. "And it's me telling you this now. Don't come looking for your parents."

"Greyland, I—"

Everything in me went numb. My eyes blinked back to reality. I was on the monorail now. Chained and gagged with Alluse around my hands.

I was going to die.

I was going to die without ever telling Lilia Evalyn Fervic how I felt about her.

EPILOGUE

Lilia

I HAD BEEN ALONE in the cabin for weeks, maybe months. I wasn't sure.

I'd made a dent in the canned food that was here, but eventually I was going to run out.

Greyland promised he was coming back for me.

He promised.

But that was forever ago. Now winter was coming in, and the constant daylight was shifting and fading into the Dark Season. It was getting colder, and I was alone.

I kept picturing him how I saw him last—beaten and shackled. The High Council had him, and I had no idea why. I didn't even know what happened to Peter. All I knew was that Sie was imprisoned, and now Greyland was captured too. And what he said about my parents—

I cried nearly every day.

Was any of it real?

I could go back. I could leave this cabin, walk back through the woods, and find Kitlarn. But then what? I didn't have any powers. The zero on my wrist kept reminding me of that. I couldn't do anything.

But I was going to die here if I stayed. When the food ran out... I was going to die, and I was alone.

I hated being alone before, but it was nothing compared to this.

I slept as much as I could, even when I wasn't tired, I tried to sleep —to dream. I wanted to sleep my life away, my worries away. I wanted to dream about *him*. And I kept wondering if I made it all up. Was my last dream of him even real? Or was that only a dream within a dream and now I was staying in a cabin worried about nothing? Maybe none of it happened. Maybe my parents thought I went missing and I was worrying them by staying here.

Maybe they were still alive.

Maybe I was crying over nothing.

Maybe I was just a coward.

I didn't trust my own mind.

I was going insane.

I *was* insane.

And alone.

There was only one thing I knew for certain, and it was that no matter how hard I tried, I never dreamed of Greyland Noren again...

ENDNOTES

Find out what happens to Greyland and Lilia in River of Lavender.

ACKNOWLEDGMENTS

To my family—Anthony and Rin. Thank you so much for always supporting me. I love you both more than I can put into words. You are my entire world and none of this would have been possible without you.

To my entire family. I could cry over how grateful I am that I have such an amazing extended family in life. I can't express how much all your support means to me. When I first published Lake of Sapphire, I was blown away by your encouragement, support, and investment in my writing. It has continued to amaze me with each new book that I write. Thank you so much from the bottom of my heart. I love you and it means the world to me. I am forever grateful.

To my mom. Thank you for always reading my books (multiple times) and listening to me talk about them for hours on end over the phone. I am so grateful you are my mom. Your support means so much to me. I love you. I love you more than anything. I love you forever. I will always love you.

To my sisters. Thank you for all your love and support. I feel so blessed to have the best siblings to ever exist (Trey included). Thank you, Kelly, for always reading my books and helping me with them— even though fantasy is not your preferred genre. Thank you, Kasey, for all your help and for all our writing nights together. They are my favorite.

To Ashlynn. I am so happy to have you as a friend. It means so much to me that you took the time to read this book—when I know you are super busy—and still give me all your feedback. I can't begin to express how much I appreciate it.

To Cassie. I'm beyond words at all the help you have given me. I don't think my writing would be the same without you. Thank you so much for everything you do for my books, but also thank you for just being the most wonderful friend a girl could ask for.

To Lana, my reading bestie. I value your opinion and trust your judgement since we love all the same books. Thank you for always reading mine. It means to the world to me.

Thank you Brittany Uller from The Author Experience for proofreading my book! Working with you was a dream, and you helped polish my book beyond what I could imagine, thank you!

To Hailey. I'm so happy I met you and now have a writer friend in Washington! Thank you for all our writing days together while I attempted to edit this book but really just talked your ear off.

To my beta readers. Thank you so much from the bottom of my heart for helping me with this entire series and for taking a chance on this side story. I love you all. Cassie Stockwell, Lana Gooch, Ashlynn Caudle, Katy Farrell, Colleen Hill, Kelly Pepper, Kasey Benjamin, Natalie Hague, Stephanie Berardi, Lisa Worthy, Mary Benjamin, Nancy Kohutka, and Carter Benjamin.

This book has been so much fun to write and dive into this world with new characters, so if you decided to take a chance and read Illusion of Hazel, thank you so much! Scotlind's story will continue with River of Lavender—and you just might get more of Greyland and Lilia too.

ALSO BY MALLORY BENJAMIN

THE ALLIUM SERIES

Lake of Sapphire

Ocean of Silver

Illusion of Hazel

River of Lavender

ABOUT THE AUTHOR

Mallory graduated from Penn State with her bachelors in nursing and has worked as a nurse for eight years before becoming a full time author and mama. You can usually find her drafting stories with her baby on her lap. And when she isn't completely consumed by fictional characters and imaginary worlds, she's spending time with her family, taking an unseemly amount of pictures of her daughter, or eating chicken wings.